HELL'S AUTO PLAZA

EDIE ROSKAM

Contents

Note from the Author

Dear Reader,

This is Book One of "The Sixth Day" thriller series. Hope you absolutely love it. If you do, connect with me afterwards.

Also, I have a FREE book for you!

See you on the other side,
-Edie Roskam

P.S. I've included a glossary for your convenience.

Prologue

7th of *Nisan*[1], 5757 (April 14, 1997)

Contractions would truncate the culmination of the sixth millennium. Empyrean readiness drills were already completed. Every unit was prepared for what to do, and where to assemble, when called. Formations had dispersed to predestined areas, but a squadron commander ordered two of his fighters to detach. They were to form a security detail around a chosen innocent. It was mission-critical. Since the matter was to remain concealed, stealth tactics must be applied so as not to draw the dissentients' ire prematurely.

The two sentinels penetrated the veil and stepped into the dome. In the astronomical twilight, dense population centers shone from the spangled terrain hundreds of kilometers below. They scanned weather systems in and around the province, but didn't discern any unusual activity.

Sentinel 1 plummeted, 2 at his heels, and they traversed the expanse toward their assigned region. When they merged with an auspicious trade wind, they swooped a distance and glided underneath the polished aluminum belly of a Boeing VIP transport aircraft. Their intersection with the flight was unremarkable in the eyes of the diverse delegation of friendlies and dissentients already aboard. After a furlong, they dropped once more through the cloud cover and decelerated for a thousand meters.

Isla Navidad[2] beach resort was in the center of the pre-dawn panorama. The sentinels sensed a disturbance at an adjacent lagoon, so they drew near to the crowded sandbar and descended further. As they leaned in, they distinguished chatter about a missing person. News reporters shouted in various dialects at a captive audience of cameras and bright bulbs. Stranded visitors complained because the blockade was on the sole route to and from the resort. Meanwhile, police ignored their protests from behind a perimeter of plastic yellow tape that read *precaución*[3].

The eastern sky brightened. Flags and buoys indicated an underwater search in progress. Fishing boats remained stationary, motors off. Beyond the mortal periphery, the observers were inconspicuous to most creatures. They hovered over the tepid water until they were sure the coast was clear.

While Sentinel 1 kept watch, his consort plunged beneath the surface without a ripple. Immersion muffled the sounds. Scuba lights twinkled in the haziness. Oxygen bubbles rose from divers in wetsuits, whose faces were partly concealed by masks and snorkels. When Sentinel 2 determined his charge wasn't there, he surfaced to meet 1 above.

They spiraled in tandem to beseech the four winds. Their upsurge generated and transmitted waves through the aqueous substance of time. The sky scrolled over the sphere, to and fro, with each forward or reversal around the axis. They probed proximate evenings and mornings within range until, at last, a harbinger traced the itinerant coordinates westward to the sea.

Two aerial beams streaked in pursuit.

---

1. *Nisan*
    The first month of the Jewish religious year. (Hebrew)
2. *Isla Navidad*
    Name of a place in Mexico. Literally, "Christmas Island." (Spanish)
3. *precaución*
    Caution. (Spanish)

ONE

Mysterious Ways

A relentless tide crashed upon the shore. The lone Tempo with Texas license plates sat parked on an asphalt strip at the edge of the deserted beach in Mexico. Its back bumper had a rectangular red decal with a single, diagonal white stripe. The driver side window was down. A sad *señorita*[1] prayed in English toward the western horizon as the morning sun rose in her rearview mirror. Tears flowed. She lifted her denim jacket sleeve to dab at her wet cheeks and dripping chin as she continued to look and listen for a resolution.

The day marched on. A couple hours before dusk—after a lengthy wait and no lifeline—she abandoned her previous hopes. She started the car and drowned her sorrows in the wah-wah electric guitar riff of an Irish rock band's song.

Leah Owers started at *Carretera Federal 83*[2]. It would be several junctions and a few days before she reached her destination in the north. She kept the car doors locked and drove all night without stopping. When she became drowsy around mid-morning, she detoured through small towns and villages until she came upon a sunlit spot in the dirt road where several passionate youths played *fútbol*[3]. She parked the car and watched. Sleep overcame her eyelids, and she didn't awaken until late afternoon.

Her road trip took her into the drier, high plains and past an endless variety of painted concrete houses. Vibrant yellows, oranges, greens, and blues. Muted colors, earth tones, and shades of white. Cinder blocks with flat roofs. Shallow roofs covered in Spanish tile. On occasion, rock exterior walls lined with glass fragments or spikes broke the skyline. When she found a *barrio*[4] with the latter, her extra sense went into overload and she wouldn't pull over to urinate or take a nap there.

On the fourth morning, she entered *Ciudad Juárez, México*[5]. Early morning bells clanged from twin towers of a neoclassical cathedral. The international city was congested under a funereal veil that sprawled along the border. She followed signs to *Puente Internacional Córdova de las Américas*[6] or, as the other side called it, The Bridge of the Americas. The new *Puente Libre*[7] was open despite ongoing construction, and she was relieved because she was out of cash. The Customs officer examined her identification and waved her through. After an absence of several months, she was back in the U.S.A. for good.

Now over the border, she could see the portentous inscription on the eastern face of the *Cerro Bola*[8] Mountain. White letters, some as tall as high-rise buildings, shouted its prophecy: *La Biblia es la Verdad. Léela.*[9] She understood, and made a mental note to heed the wisdom.

After ten kilometers on I-10, she took an exit and turned on a few side streets. Then she rolled through a middle class residential neighborhood and parked in front of her favorite dwelling on that side of eternity. A police cruiser was parked in the driveway.

She honked the car horn twice.

Leah was weary from her journey, and parched. She opened the car door and stood up. The polyester-cotton blend of her floral summer dress clung to the prominent bulge around her middle. Her cousin, Susie, ran outside to welcome her. Susie's husband, Ralph, and shy little Hannah and Sofia stayed by their front door.

"It's so good to see you, Leah," Susie greeted, and they hugged each other tightly. Susie took her hand and led her into the house. Ralph went to retrieve Leah's bags from the car once everyone was inside.

Summer (1997)

LEAH HELD her newborn as the band played on. She sat beside Susie and Ralph in a large sanctuary amidst an audience of five hundred other spectators. It had been ages since she'd been to a service, and she wouldn't have gone if her cousins hadn't invited her. Thankfully, the well-lit center stage drew all the attention so she was practically invisible.

Her nervous fingers reached up to remove a wisp of long hair that had fallen in front of her eyes. She tucked it behind her left ear.

Many years prior, at her former church, there had been two scandals back-to-back that split the body in half. A popular pastor confessed to an affair with a young man he'd counseled. When a majority vote ejected him from leadership more for the homosexual act than for the actual adultery, he and his lover fled El Paso County. Inconsolable, his wife chose suicide over the void he'd left behind. It took the pastoral search committee eight weeks to recruit the next one.

Not long after the new pastor settled in, a deacon purportedly saw a dirty magazine in his study. To make matters worse, the church secretary came forward with allegations of repeated harassment by the pastor's domineering wife. The pastor insisted the pornographic literature belonged to the previous tenant, and only repented that he didn't remove the item from his environment as expeditiously as he should have.

His wife dutifully backed his story. As for the harassment, the couple claimed the secretary misunderstood her playful sense of humor. She'd certainly never propose a *ménage à trois*[10] with anyone, at least not seriously, and they apologized for the offense. Several married couples believed them, but many doubted. There was malicious gossip and infighting behind the scenes as the pastor continued to preach from the pulpit every weekend.

Eventually, backbiting engulfed the congregation and brother turned against brother. The usually laughter-filled, fun-loving youth group also divided into factions. Relationships cooled. Leah had given up on church after that. Her tender teenage heart never mended from the ordeal.

The song ended and the sanctuary lights turned up. Leah shifted in her seat. Singers and musicians exited, and the audience clapped politely as a sharp-dressed, elder preacher with a chestnut toupee walked on stage. He placed a large black Bible on the lectern and quoted a verse from memory.

"The thief," he intoned, "comes to steal, and kill, and destroy."

The crowd was breathless to hear the rest.

"But I came," the old preacher continued, "that you may have and enjoy life. A life filled with abundance!"

"Amen," affirmed a vivacious, grandmotherly member in a powder blue, wide-brimmed hat.

"Do you want your life to be filled to the top?" he explored, both arms extended to his sides. "And spilling over with good things?"

The audience broke into exuberant applause. Television cameras panned and swiveled to capture several audible declarations of faith.

The preacher's prosperity message made Leah's ears perk up. She was desperate for a sense of peace and security. Her checking account balance was close to zero. Blessings seemed elusive but that man seemed to have the answers.

She listened intently to his teachings.

---

1. *señorita*
   An unmarried woman. (Spanish)
2. *Carretera Federal 83*
   Federal Highway 83 in Mexico. (Spanish)
3. *fútbol*
   Soccer. (Spanish)
4. *barrio*
   Neighborhood. (Spanish)
5. *Ciudad Juárez, México*
   City of Juarez, Mexico. (Spanish)
6. *Puente Internacional Córdova de las Américas*
   Cordova International Bridge of the Americas. (Spanish)
7. *Puente Libre*
   Free Bridge. (Spanish)
8. *Cerro Bola*
   Name of a mountain in Mexico. Literally, "ball hill." (Spanish)
9. *La Biblia es la Verdad. Léela.*
   The Bible is the Truth. Read it. (Spanish)
10. *ménage à trois*
    An arrangement in which three people share a sexual relationship. (French)

TWO

Tree of Knowledge

Friday, the 13th (February 1998)

The rusted Tempo, with a red scuba flag decal on its back bumper, slowed and turned at the entrance to Prince Auto Plaza. It proceeded past two rubbernecking smokers on the colonnade. The salesmen had strategically planted themselves by a column closest to the entrance from the customer parking lot.

Leah pulled into an open space. The car's dashboard clock and her ticking wristwatch agreed she was fifteen minutes early. She clicked off her seatbelt and checked the vanity mirror.

The advertisement stated Potential Six Figure Income. Since the average household in El Paso brought in thirty thousand dollars annually, landing that job would change her trajectory. She must convince the boss man she could do it.

Her nerves were frazzled, so she breathed out slowly to

help settle them and concentrated on positive thoughts. The abundant life, the old preacher taught, was for those who had a big faith. And faith was only possible when negativity was expelled.

She traded her aqua blue flip-flops for a borrowed pair of nude heels. After she tossed important documents into a tan tote bag, she quickly exited the car before she could lose the courage.

Her high heels struggled to stay vertical on the asphalt surface. When she finally reached the smooth concrete portico, the same two human smokestacks awaited her arrival. The senior salesperson's black cap bore the crest of a bird of prey.

"Hello," said Mr. Jameson. "Is there someone I can help you find?"

"Yes, Will Housely. I'm here for an interview."

The younger salesperson turned away as soon as he learned she wasn't an automotive retail customer.

A few moments later, Leah sat in the customer waiting area in the showroom beside the service drive. She was on one end of a plush sectional in front of a colorful fish aquarium. Enigmatic notes of a song by an early eighties English rock band floated in the spacious chamber above her head. The front man sang spiteful lyrics about a reversal of fortune and power.

Meanwhile, senior salesperson Mr. Jameson conferred with a pretty head chock-full of highlights. The faceless woman was seated behind the reception desk.

Leah peered into the fish tank. A miniature scuba diver leaked tiny air bubbles, which escaped to the surface. He was perched on the sparkly rocks next to a pirate's chest filled with gold coins. She imagined she was the diver who'd found hidden treasure at the bottom of the sea. Now all she needed was to find a way to haul it to shore.

She looked at her surroundings. The showroom was a tall box with mostly glass on the eastern half that faced the street. Framed prints on surrounding walls depicted contemporaries of Julius Caesar, the Parthenon, and Roman architecture. Grecian style planters were tastefully arrayed throughout. One pedestal was a sculpture of Maenads, the three female worshippers of Dionysus.

There was a whiff of burning rubber with a hint of nail polish remover. She counted one, two, three American-made vehicles on center display, parked parallel and equidistant over a polished, white marble floor. Oak desks, a couple of round tables, and cubicles were lined up at the sides. A raised platform, which resembled a judge's bench, dominated the corner by the main entry. Its wood panels reminded her of the partition between lectern and choir loft in a church's chancel area.

From that vantage point, she could observe much of the dealership's front activity. Employees walked with purpose in a rehearsed choreography that crisscrossed the showroom. Most held something in their hands. Other worker bees filled distinct six-sided cells in the grand honeycomb. She couldn't help but wonder where the gooey golden center of the hive was located.

The bearded man in a stained uniform finished an explanation about a dirty air filter to the couple seated by the stairs. He withdrew and walked toward the service drive. A stocky man in a shimmery maroon suit walked casually next to the row of desks along the wall of floor-to-ceiling windows. He looked behind him and to the side at some cubicles while he tucked a couple of manila folders under one arm. Then, with a sudden jerk to the right, he was out a side door like a fugitive.

Leah blinked and puzzled over that for half a minute.

Her eyes refocused on a lady in a tight black dress who

walked slowly and provocatively up the stairs that led to a series of glass cube offices on the second floor. Then she saw a striking, middle-aged man appear in one of the upper level windows. He looked like a Greek male model with his raven hair and midnight blue Armani suit, and he appeared to revel in the moment. From that vantage point, Leah figured, Tommy Prince could see more of his empire than she could. She recognized him from the TV commercials, and hoped she'd get a chance to meet him.

Promptly at ten o'clock, the General Manager met her with a firm, dry handshake. William Housely was a pointy faced, fifty-year-old with sideburns that attached to his mustache. He led the way to an open desk on the showroom floor and offered to get her a bottled water. They settled into an easy banter about her work experience as a dive instructor at *Isla Navidad*[1] Resort in Mexico. He went on to review the attendance requirements, and the dealership's stair step compensation that rewarded both volume and gross.

Since she didn't have a client base yet, Housely told her he didn't expect her to earn more than eighty thousand in her first year. However, if she were to build a network of referrals, it would make all the difference between year one and year two. She could expect to earn six figures then. He said he could think of a few sales consultants who netted more last year than his physician did.

Leah tried not to look too impressed as she asked what she could do to set herself apart as they had.

"The car business takes grit. Have you ever done anything difficult?"

She needed to mention something other than giving birth to Beka.

"PADI certification."

"What's that?"

"Rescue diver training. It was rigorous."

"When was this?"

"A couple years ago, before I had my daughter."

His eyes narrowed slightly.

"As I mentioned earlier, this job is bell-to-bell. Six days a week."

"It won't be an issue."

"Who will care for your child when you have customers after 10 p.m.?"

"My cousin, Susie. She homeschools her kids and we live with them. I won't have any daycare worries."

"How do you feel about working with men?"

"I don't mind."

Housely tapped the desk with two fingers.

She laughed.

"Working with salesmen might be easier than working with some women I've known."

He responded with a toothy grin.

"Fair enough. I want you to stay right there. I'd like you to meet somebody."

Several minutes passed. Leah attempted to appear subdued as a white-haired man walked by and gawked over his spectacles at her chest. After he passed, she felt her shirt buttons just in case any had popped open. *Nope.* They were still secure.

Housely reappeared and proudly introduced their Used Car Director, Moose. He was mostly hairless, and slightly shorter than his boss. Leah stood for the handshake. Housely boasted that Moose Stalwart was hands-down the best used car guy in all of Texas, New Mexico, and Arizona. Then he left to give them privacy.

During their brief conversation, Stalwart told Leah the nickname Moose started as an inside joke during his college football days. He confessed he'd worked with

Housely for decades. Stalwart also revealed that his ex-wife was Housely's sister.

Although Leah was a bit intimidated by him at first, Stalwart turned out to be more mouse than moose. He was rather soft-spoken and reserved for a man who reportedly ascended the ranks and reached the pinnacle of sales performance in three states. It gave her hope.

She leaned in with fascination and genuinely wanted to hear more. However, she sensed he was preoccupied. As he stared over her head toward the other end of the building, his pink cheeks increased a shade. She'd need to get that man's attention, and gain his approval, so he'd recommend her to Housely.

"Tell me how to build a successful career at Prince Auto."

He redirected his gaze to her neckline.

"Be so valuable they can never replace you."

She pictured the wealth she'd attain after a few years under that man's mentorship.

Right on time, Housely returned and, as the two men traded places, Stalwart muttered something into Housely's ear. To her, it sounded disturbingly like a string of expletives. Stalwart's face was now bright red, but he managed to nod a polite adieu in her direction. He walked rapidly away toward the wood platform by the front doors.

Her eyes followed him and stopped when she thought she saw a gory splatter on the far wall over the platform area. Apparently, Stalwart needed to hurriedly rub his guilty stains out of existence before anyone investigated. She hadn't had one of those visions in a while, and blinked slowly to extinguish it.

"Sell me this pen."

Suddenly, Housely held an average black ballpoint pen over the desk between them.

Her mind whirled.

"Take it."

She did, and tried to think of how to begin.

"This pen is manufactured by Bic Incorporated. They have a wonderful reputation because they make reliable pens. They've been around for fifty years. Or maybe more, I don't know."

"Go on."

"This particular pen is a ballpoint. The rollerball glides smoothly to distribute the ink evenly across the paper. See?"

She flipped over her résumé and demonstrated an elegant loop on the back page.

"Now, you try."

She handed over the pen, and he scribbled in cursive.

"It won't leave behind any blotches. That's our guarantee. We offer ballpoints in black, blue, and red. As you can see, the cap color indicates the color of the ink."

She gulped for air.

"Ballpoints have a finer stroke compared to our felt-tip and gel pens. You'll notice this pen doesn't retract but, if that's a feature you want, I can get you one that does. We have a retractable with four different ink colors in one. Is that something that interests you?"

Housely pushed his chair back and stood.

"Leia, thank you for coming in."

"Leah. Rhymes with See-Ya."

"Ah, that's right. Lee-Ya."

"I really appreciate this opportunity."

"It was good to meet you. I'll be in touch."

They shook hands once again and she turned to leave. She had a good feeling.

Her heels clicked through the cavernous showroom. The appearance of several curious onlookers made her conscious of the sounds she made. She didn't want to interrupt their workflow, but she didn't see more than two or three customers in the vicinity. Perhaps the sales representatives only wanted to assess her threat level. If that were the case, she shouldn't let them know she didn't have previous sales experience.

She held her head high, and pretended to possess the confidence of a highly qualified candidate. One who'd just easily landed a lucrative job offer. Housely would simply have to wait by the phone while she took her time to decide whether or not she'd accept.

As she walked through the huge glass doors she'd entered an hour prior, she saw Mr. Jameson and the other smoker were no longer outside. They must have found more rewarding employment elsewhere. Their replacement was a fidgety young man about her age. He tucked an escaped white shirttail into loose khaki pants that fell at the hips. She did a double take at the remains of his scraggly red tie. Someone had cut it off just a few centimeters below his Adam's apple.

He froze in place. A lit cigarette dangled from his unnaturally crimson grin.

She gave him a wide berth and picked up the pace.

---

1. *Isla Navidad*
    Name of a place in Mexico. Literally, "Christmas Island." (Spanish)

THREE

Indoctrination

The next day, Leah called Prince Auto Plaza to express her continued interest in the sales consultant position. Housely said he hadn't made a decision yet. He promised to call her when he did.

She waited tables part-time at the pancake house during the breakfast rush and scraped up meager tips. A week passed, and she was almost at her wits' end. She tried so hard to think only positive thoughts but, in the dead silence, she chewed over the ways she'd potentially sabotaged herself in the interview.

Those automotive pros must have thought she sounded like an idiot.

With her lack of higher education, the sales job was a rare chance to earn a significant income and put away a nest egg. Susie and Ralph were supportive, as usual, but they expressed concern centered on the stigma of a car sales career. They said they were certain she'd have a tough road ahead, but she also might never get married if she didn't settle for a more suitable form of employment. In a moment of weakness, she retorted that she wasn't on the prowl for a husband and she certainly didn't need a man to provide for her.

She apologized for the outburst, and her cousins quickly forgave her.

Leah had the deepest appreciation for them. They'd been so compassionate and patient about her unplanned pregnancy; she surely didn't want to overstay her welcome. If she hadn't been at the end of her rope, she wouldn't have asked for help.

Intensely determined to become self-reliant again, she set a deadline to be out of their house and back on her own. One year. By the end of next February. She and Beka would move into an apartment or a modest house.

She swore to herself that she'd start to pay Susie for monthly rent if Prince Auto Plaza hired her. Correction: *when* she received her first paycheck from Prince Auto Plaza. Old Preacher Johnson taught that thoughts and spoken words created reality.

Friday and Saturday came and went without a word. On Sunday afternoon, while everyone else was out of the house, she sat with Beka on the soft beige carpet in the living room. Her mind returned to the interview and she cringed once more. Then the cordless phone on the end table rang.

She scrambled to check the Caller ID. It was Prince Auto Plaza's number.

WILL HOUSELY'S phone call on Sunday gave her enough time to give the burned out pancake house Manager a facial tic and one-week notice.

Housely had explained to her that he'd fly in a renowned sales trainer and automotive veteran to give her the absolute best chance of success. Randall Fenton would introduce the traditional Road-to-the-Sale process followed by everyone who was anyone in the car business. Although Prince Auto would fully compensate Randall at the end of the week, they'd consider a portion of his fees a short-term loan to each of the new hires. Each candidate who passed the test at the end of the course could stay on as a full-time sales consultant, with the agreement that Prince Auto would deduct fifty dollars from the first paycheck and each of four consecutive pay periods until the debt was fully paid.

It was now Monday morning. Her first morning at Prince Auto. Leah felt a twinge as she remembered there was a remote possibility she wouldn't have a job at the end of the week. A cloud of gloom and doom hung over her head. She breathed deeply.

I'm a winner.

Besides, she'd never fail any test she studied for.

The training class was in a room located toward the back of the palatial dealership's upper level. Over two dozen cherry stained plaques lined a wall. Each represented a calendar year in Prince Auto Plaza's legacy, and uniform metal plates were engraved with names of illustrious Salespersons of the Month. She scanned but didn't find Housely, Stalwart, or a Prince family member listed.

Leah sat with three other recruits, two men and one woman, around a massive vintage mahogany conference table. A black carry-on sat in the corner. Everyone assumed it belonged to their soon-to-be-mentor and, therefore, he must already be somewhere in the building. They put on their nametags, and made a sincere effort to get to know one another as they waited for Randall Fenton.

Chuck was a slender, short man over thirty with a thick, black mustache. His grey suit fit as if it had been perfectly tailored to his frame. He and his wife Linda had five small children. The Army Reserves helped pay the bills. His previous sales experience involved vacuum cleaners and household furniture, and his facial expressions were animated.

Sandra was a postmenopausal woman with short, salt and pepper hair. She looked very serious in her navy blue pantsuit and pearls. She worked as an executive secretary in the sixties, until she married the executive. They raised two children to adulthood. Late last year, her husband left her for another woman who was their daughter's age. Although she won the house in the divorce settlement, her ex-husband didn't support her financially. She needed a job to pay property tax and the remainder of her mortgage payments.

Then there was Marvin, an affable and at ease young bachelor about Leah's age. Even though he was a college dropout, he asked good questions and truly listened to everyone's answers. His white shirt and grey silk tie were birthday gifts from his awesome girlfriend. Lifelong friends were back for a visit and he'd already made plans to hang with them next weekend.

Housely came in to announce Randall Fenton.

The sales trainer bounded into the room like a legendary rock star who might need to do another round at rehab. His flabby stomach drooped over his belt buckle and his fleshy body indicated a man who had never worked a day of hard labor in his life. He high fived everyone. Marvin let out a whoop and offered two palms up top.

Randall landed at the end of the conference table, smiled broadly, and complimented the good-looking group. He thanked Housely, who still stood by the door, for the invitation to the Sun City to spend a week with them. Everyone turned toward the General Manager as he acknowledged Randall's gratitude with a nod. He said he knew the group was in excellent hands.

When he turned to leave, Randall smoothly resumed control of the room.

Their sales instructor began with an introduction of his humble beginnings, and listed major accomplishments that led to his near-celebrity status within the automotive industry. All was due to his mastery of the Road-to-the-Sale. He mesmerized them with his story, infecting them with his positive energy.

As evidence of his proudest achievements, he reached into his carry-on and brought out a small album: photographs of himself in front of a lake house, at a grill on the back of a cruiser boat, by the Eiffel Tower with a glamorous female companion, in the driver's seat of a European roadster, and with half a dozen cute children purported to be his progeny. Leah thought the photos looked to be about twenty years old, as she could best determine by the perms, outdated fashions, and the vast difference in his waistline.

Randall also retrieved and passed out black binders that contained the curriculum. Those valuable copies were for classroom use only. The students were not to write in them. Instead, they were to jot down their notes on yellow legal pads the dealership provided. He told them he wanted the binders returned immediately after they completed their open book exams on Friday.

They turned to the summary page:
Road-to-the-Sale

- Proper Meet and Greet
- Fact Finding
- Select a Vehicle from Stock

- World Class Product Presentation and Demonstration Drive
- Trade Evaluation
- Getting Seated and Relaxed
- Trial Close[1]
- Write Up
- Negotiate and Close
- Proper Turn to the Business Office[2]
- Proper Delivery
- Follow Up After the Sale

"NOW," Randall transitioned. "Think of a personal challenge."

One by one, every face around the conference table pondered their challenges. Sandra glanced at Leah and then looked down at her own hands.

"What would you say if I told you I, Randall Fenton, can solve your problems?"

Chuck openly balked at his claim.

"I'm serious. I can tell you the one thing you need. There's only one correct answer. One solution to any problem."

Leah thought that sounded vaguely familiar but he didn't strike her as the religious type. She hesitated.

"Do you want to know what the answer is?"

Chuck raised his bushy black eyebrows.

Sandra's expression remained flat.

"Tell us!" Marvin implored.

"Anyone want to take a stab at it?"

"Money."

Everyone looked at Sandra.

"Yes! Money is the answer."

Leah was so glad she hadn't spoken up. That wasn't the time, nor the place, to look foolish and recount cherished memories of one summer at youth camp.

"Chuck, what was your last argument with your wife about?"

"She wanted to buy the kids rollerblades and Air Jordans."

"What's wrong with that?"

"The timing wasn't right. We didn't know what our tax refund was going to be and the rent was due."

"So, you had to make a choice. What if money wasn't a problem?"

"Then she could buy whatever she wants. I'd never say no."

Randall rubbed his hands together and bobbed his head up and down in hearty agreement.

"Marvin, do you have a student loan?"

"Yes, I have a few."

"May I inquire how much you owe?"

"Forty-two thousand."

Chuck let out a low whistle.

Leah was shocked.

"It's a good thing I quit before I started medical school."

"What happens if you can't make a payment?"

"I'd have to pay the balance."

"Can you afford that?"

"If I had forty-two thousand stashed away in my loveseat, I wouldn't be in this class."

Randall paced back and forth.

"You have to make the payments, or it will ding your credit score."

Marvin nodded.

"So, if you netted an extra, say, fifty thousand this year: What would you do with it?"

"I'd use half of it to pay down the loans. Then I'd take my girlfriend on vacation to Japan and pop the question."

"I bet she'd like that."

Sandra sneered.

"Leah, can you tell me about a challenge you're experiencing right now?"

OVER THE NEXT SEVENTY-TWO HOURS, Randall immersed them into the twelve steps that would earn them more in commissions and bonuses than they'd ever dreamed. He said he expected their full participation in role-play. They shouldn't have stage fright when it was time to hit the hot asphalt.

"Check your inhibitions at the door."

Every day at noon, two young salesmen in dress shirts and ties delivered a deli platter, bags of chips, and a cooler filled with canned sodas and bottled water. The teacher and his students would eat their lunches and share small talk around the table. Randall would invariably reach into his black carry-on and pull out a sandwich bag filled with pills. When Leah finally asked about them, he mentioned his wife sold supplements as a hobby and he was impressed with the results so far. They boosted his afternoon energy levels, even when he was jet lagged, and he claimed to have lost twelve pounds in one week. He wrote his name on a few of his wife's business cards and handed them out.

That week, Leah and her classmates practiced a new lingo. Randall took care to introduce car business terms like up[3] (a customer who walked on the car lot), trade walk[4], test drive[5], sold lane[6], first pencil[7], MSRP[8], sales tower[9], close, deal jacket[10], F&I[11], due bill[12], and business office. When a customer owed more than their trade-in vehicle was worth, he described their situation as upside down[13], or negative equity[14]. He warned that seasoned sales consultants and Managers might use other terms, like underwater[15] or buried[16], but he frowned upon the use of death imagery whenever prospects and customers were within earshot.

He insisted that sales professionals always maintained control of the sales process and built momentum. They should be upbeat and never allow customers to become mentally stuck in the details.

On Thursday, he treated the class to a special lunch out at an Italian restaurant. Once the group returned to the dealership, they hunkered down for an intensive review and open Q&A session. The test scheduled for the next day would be multiple choice with an essay question at the end.

First thing on Friday morning, Marvin the bachelor came in to say goodbye. He'd accepted another offer. He was to manage his friend's adult video store on the eastside. The job started at twenty bucks an hour, plus bonuses, and he simply couldn't refuse that kind of generosity. Randall wished him well and said he knew not everyone had the stomach for commission-only sales.

Leah was always an excellent student in school, and naturally competitive, so she was the first to turn in her exam during the allotted two hours. Randall graded her test. Of course, she passed, as did Chuck and Sandra. After Housely received the results, he came in to congratulate them and extend a warm welcome to the Prince Auto team. Then he went to retrieve the Office Manager who would prepare all the new hire paperwork.

Randall packed the four black binders. A serene expression settled on his chubby face. He seemed happy for his graduates. When he'd said his goodbyes, he solemnly shook their hands one last time and exited the room without any fanfare.

As they waited for the Office Manager, Leah instinctively got up and sped out the door to catch him. Even before he'd taken his afternoon pills, the man was already down the stairs and past the sales tower. He waved at the Sales Managers and they waved back. Then he walked out the oversized showroom doors and towed his small black suitcase behind him.

A couple of smokers outside ogled Leah's body but she decided she'd have more time to properly address that issue later. She fell into step beside Randall and he turned toward her. Recognition washed over his face. They continued the walk to his rental car, which he'd parked near the curb. He opened the trunk and placed his suitcase next to a matching garment bag. Obviously, he was on his way to the airport and she might never see him again. She thanked him for all the valuable lessons, and gave him a hug.

Before they parted, he held her shoulder with a firm grip and gave the benediction.

"May you have one Hell of a successful car business career."

Then he reached around and smacked her on the rear.

––––––––––––––––––––

1. close
     Term to describe the act of convincing a customer to agree to a sales transaction.
2. business office
     Slang used to describe the area or office where F&I managers work.
3. up
     A customer who walks on the lot.
4. trade walk

A term used to describe when a salesperson takes the customer around the trade vehicle and silently examines its flaws.

5. test drive

Driving of a motor vehicle to determine its drivability or road-worthiness, and general operating state.

6. sold lane

A spot a salesperson will ask the customer to park after a test drive, as a soft close technique.

7. first pencil

The opening offer from a sales manager, often written onto the four-square worksheet.

8. MSRP

Manufacturer's Suggested Retail Price.

9. sales tower

Term used to describe where the sales managers sit when penciling deals.

10. deal jacket

A folder that contains all the information in a customer's transaction.

11. F&I

An acronym for Finance and Insurance.

12. due bill

A document to describe work promised or outstanding obligations.

13. upside down

A term to describe the condition of owing more than a vehicle's worth.

14. negative equity

A term to describe the condition of owing more than a vehicle's worth.

15. underwater

A term to describe the condition of owing more than a vehicle's worth.

16. buried

A term to describe the condition of owing much more than a vehicle's worth.

Hocus Pocus

Leah strolled through the large oversized glass doors and carried a high stack of homemade walnut brownies covered with plastic wrap. She left the plate at the reception desk with Valerie, the middle-age woman with thick highlights in her hair.

The reason for celebration was it was Leah's first Saturday morning at Prince Auto Plaza and, according to Housely, Saturday was the busiest day of the work week. He said they'd be open Sundays as well if it weren't for the Texas Blue Law.

A few dozen sales and finance department employees jammed into the upstairs conference room at 7:20 for the weekend kickoff meeting. From the doorway, it appeared to be standing room only. A few people held steamy Styrofoam cups and everyone listened to an old boom box play crackly eighties rock on the Q while they waited for the real action to begin.

When Leah went in, she saw she could join Chuck and Sandra at the table. Most chairs were unoccupied. It seemed almost taboo for the newbies to sit down, so they asked around. The white-haired man insisted it was okay.

Leah sat between Sandra and white-haired Howard. She'd seen the Fleet Manager several times around the showroom with a clipboard. He looked over his bifocals at her like she was the subject of an inhumane experiment at Auschwitz. He explained that Managers and sales veterans would remain standing, but anyone who sat down was generally a newcomer or a woman. He said he had to sit because of his trick knee. Then he turned his chair toward Leah and talked as if they were old acquaintances.

He came off a bit smarmy and it gave her an unpleasant feeling. She noticed he didn't wear an under-shirt, either. When he scratched his crotch with dingy fingernails, as if she didn't have eyes to see, she turned away and silently prayed for the meeting to begin.

Before long, a lady entered the conference room. Leah had seen her in a similar tight black dress before. Now, she carried a silver tray topped with envelopes and a pair of dice. Housely and Stalwart followed her in. The team reacted with hoots and hollers, clapped in rhythm, and chanted:

"Moose. Moose. Moose."

Stalwart shouted names and numbers from a list as a junior Sales Manager scribbled on the dry erase board. He wrote last names of sales consultants, followed by the number of eligible units each individual sold in the previous six days. The names were listed from most to least number of units, and ordered based on gross profit. Every name had sold at least one unit.

The number of envelopes matched the number of sales consultants on the board. Each envelope held cash in varying totals from one hundred up to five hundred dollars, but one envelope was supposed to contain one thousand five hundred dollars. The envelopes were marked with random numbers from three through ten, and the Managers guaranteed the jackpot was in an envelope marked with a ten. On that morning, there were two envelopes with a ten so only one of those would contain the jackpot.

According to the rules, a sales consultant could select an envelope marked with a ten only if he rolled a ten. If he didn't roll that sum, he could choose to roll again as many times as he was allowed based on his number of sales. Or he could accept whatever number came up and grab an envelope with that number written on it. If the sales consultant rolled a number over ten, it didn't count. If he rolled snake eyes, he lost his turn and had to wait until everyone else went.

The lady blew on the game dice and someone in the room let out a slow wolf howl. Another whistled. She handed them to the player whose name was at the top of the list.

The sales consultant had a number four on the board so he could roll up to four times if he wanted. When he rolled a ten on his very first attempt, it caused a panic. His co-workers pounded their fists on the table, chairs, and other surfaces as Lady Luck walked over to him with the silver tray and he carefully selected one of the two envelopes marked ten. The other players agonized as he unhurriedly tore it open and counted what was inside: two hundred fifty dollars.

Pandemonium erupted and quickly died down.

Now everyone knew, without a doubt, the other envelope marked with a ten contained the jackpot. The junior Sales Manager recorded the dollar amount on the board next to the sales consultant's name.

The next guy rolled a six. He rolled again and ended

up with another six on his final turn. He selected an envelope marked with a six and counted four hundred twenty-five dollars. He kissed it and crossed himself, as the junior Sales Manager recorded the amount on the board.

From a far corner, a Manager in a three-piece suit raised his voice over the loud music to remind everyone they were not to leave the room until they signed their bonus receipts.

There were boos when a competitor's commercial came on the radio, so Chuck turned off the boom box.

The game of chance ensued and spirits became lively again. Finally, the last salesperson stepped forward with a smug look. The only envelope that remained was marked with a ten.

All havoc broke loose.

Sandra covered her ears due to the thunderous ovation.

The lucky sales consultant had rolled snake eyes on a previous turn, so he'd waited for everyone else to go ahead. The rules of the game didn't require a roll for the last envelope; the one thousand five hundred dollar jackpot was his.

Leah laughed aloud with amusement.

Chuck slow-clapped and shook his head in disbelief.

The sales consultant opened the envelope, counted out fifteen crisp C-notes, and kissed Lady Luck full on the mouth. She didn't resist.

Housely stepped forward to announce to everyone's extreme pleasure that he'd extend the bonus incentive through Friday and they'd repeat the dice game next Saturday. He passed out the new list of qualifiers, since so many vehicles had fallen off the previous. He reminded everyone he'd spiff a hundred dollars for a hat trick[1], which he defined for the sake of newcomers as when a salesperson sold three units in a day. He described it as cash-in-fist[2] and money that Momma doesn't need to know about[3]. To Leah, that sounded like a cash payout that didn't leave a paper trail.

He proceeded to give a motivational speech like a coach at half time. There was a lot of crosstalk in the room but Leah quickly apprehended it was by design. He'd call out to individuals about some great plays he noticed they made during the past week, and they'd answer back in the affirmative. There would be applause whenever a sales consultant's efforts were lauded. Often, a fellow consultant or a Manager would further acknowledge the person's achievement with a nudge, fist bump, or slap on the back.

Housely bragged that one of the green peas closed[4] a Momma's boy[5] on a five-pounder[6] and now it was over the curb[7]. He credited F&I[8] Director, Gerald Allen, for hammering[9] the bank and getting it done. There was so much slang Leah was absolutely certain Randall had never uttered in class, but she caught on to most of it and wrote the rest in her notebook: T.O.[10], cockroach[11], lay down[12], stroke[13], skate[14], split[15], weak[16], strong[17], code four[18], silver hair[19], and ducks on the pond[20].

Before they dismissed, the junior Sales Manager went around and collected signed receipts. Housely introduced the three recruits and asked everyone to be lenient as they got accustomed to their roles. A smatter of laughter went around the room. Leah was surprised by a few hostile looks in the crowd, but chalked it up to their fiercely competitive natures.

Housely nodded to Stalwart, who called on a senior sales consultant named Reverend Bobby Dean who had the drawl of a southern preacher. Everyone joined his recitation of the mantra with a masculine shout from their diaphragms:

"O Fortune, smile. On Montana motor mile. This is what we pray. Bless us every day."

Then the sales meeting emptied faster than Sunday churchgoers out to beat the lunch crowd.

SINCE LEAH HADN'T SCHEDULED any customer appointments, Housely assigned her to shadow Mr. Jameson. She could tell right away the senior sales consultant wasn't thrilled to have her hang around him all day. Every effort was exerted to maintain a respectful distance and, when the sales department's order of twenty pizzas arrived at noon, she brought him a couple of slices with an ice-cold bottled water.

His sour face softened a bit after that.

Mid-afternoon rolled around, and it was Mr. Jameson's turn at the up point[21] pillar again. A black 4-door sedan drove in and two women, a fifty-year-old and her adult daughter, stepped out. They looked over to the new SUVs.

He approached them and followed the *modus operandi*[22]. The mother said she'd seen a red midsize SUV in traffic and she wanted to take a closer look. He showed them the lineup, to select one from, but none of the vehicles really stood out.

Mr. Jameson inquired about their monthly payment range, so he could help them select the right SUV for their budget. When they told him their thoughts, he shook his head and took a step back to review the long line of midsize SUVs. Then he told them he remembered there was supposed to be a marked down unit. He searched again but couldn't find it. He asked if they'd mind a short wait while he retrieved it from the back lot. They said they wouldn't mind, so he seated them in the customer waiting area and told Leah to remain with them. He promised to return shortly.

Fifteen minutes later, Mr. Jameson led them into the garage. It was completely dark in there because the service department closed early on Saturdays. He flipped a switch on the wall and a single bulb illumined from the high ceiling.

Awash in glittery spotlight, directly below, posed a new midsize SUV in Yuletide Red. Leah thought she could hear the unseasonal sound of distant sleigh bells. Melodious organ music started up, immediately accompanied by the syncopated rhythms of a gospel medley. The customers must have heard it too, because they busted out a few choir dance moves and didn't need any more persuasion.

After their test drive[23], they agreed to terms as Mr. Jameson presented on the first pencil[24].

ALTHOUGH LEAH DIDN'T HAVE a chance to make any of her own deals happen on Saturday, she felt Sunday would be full of promise. She showed up at the closed dealership loaded with blank business cards and a positive attitude. Several people browsed the new and used inventories undisturbed. Some came alone, but most had a friend or a spouse.

When she approached and introduced herself, many expressed surprise that she was an automotive sales consultant. She was able to convince three prospects to give her their phone numbers. She promised to do her very best to make them happy customers. She meant every word she said.

Sometime during the two hours she stayed, a white Jeep Wrangler drove in and parked beside the portico. A young man in blue jeans and a pair of ropers got out and, a minute later, a contractor van arrived and parked behind him. He unlocked the doors for workers in coveralls.

She thought the latter might be electricians. Maybe they were there to service the alarm system.

The men were still in the building when she left at noon.

ON HER WAY to the house, Leah stopped by a Vietnamese restaurant and picked up an order of spring rolls with spicy peanut sauce. Her plan was to trade them for Beka.

When she walked in, Susie was at the breakfast table and still dressed in her church clothes. Susie held Beka over her lap so she appeared to be standing on her own, but her little toes barely touched. The baby was enamored with something over the woman's head.

Leah placed the to-go box in front of her cousin.

"My favorite?"

"Yeah. How was church?"

"Good. The sermon was about the lion's den."

"Where are Ralph and the girls?"

"They went to visit Savannah the Elephant."

"You deserve to treat yourself."

"I might give myself a pedicure. After I take a nap."

Susie relinquished Beka and opened the box.

Leah held her daughter close, and breathed in her irresistible baby scent. Beka had a yellow band in her soft hair, and wore an adorable sunflower top and pink tutu. She gave a toothless grin and made happy baby noises when her young mother covered her face with wet kisses.

"I'm taking her out for ice cream."

"Mm-hmm. Have fun."

Leah retrieved the car seat and diaper bag from a nearby stool.

"And, after that, Beka and Mommy are going to the park."

They disappeared through the doorway.

IT WAS A WARM, sunny day. The ice cream shop bustled with customers. Leah walked inside with comfortable flip-flops on her feet, and barefoot Beka slung over one hip. A large family waited impatiently for their turn. She took a number at the counter and peered through the frosty glass at the flavor selection.

Her standby had always been Nutty Coconut, but it would be Beka's first time. She couldn't wait to see her facial expression.

"Leah?"

She turned to see a tall man with glasses. He looked like a statesman who pressed flesh with constituents on casual Sunday afternoons. Where had she seen him before?

"It's me, Henry Martin."

He wore a polo shirt that bore Prince Auto's logo. He resembled the Manager in Saturday's sales meeting who'd worn a three-piece suit.

"Henry! You look so different. I almost didn't recognize you."

"This is my family."

He moved aside to introduce his wife, Janet, who had flawless skin and didn't need makeup. Then Leah met their slightly disheveled troupe of boys and girls ages four through ten. Each child wore remarkably clean clothes.

"You have eight children?"

Janet smiled, and rubbed Beka's chubby arm.

"We're foster parents," Henry stated.

It was the Martins' turn to get their ice cream. Janet handled her children like a drill sergeant. While their father ordered ten single-scoop vanilla cones, they sat and clasped their hands in their laps.

When Leah's turn came around, she helped Beka to sample Old Fashioned Vanilla, Chocolate, and Strawberry Sherbet. The last flavor puckered the baby's lips and her little body shivered with delight. Leah laughed through tears and requested a double scoop in a to-go cup.

She looked back at the Martin troupe.

The children enjoyed their treats and their parents doted on them. Janet and the eldest girl monitored the youngest girl's progress. At the other end, Henry told jokes to two boys with curly hair. With a sudden look of astonishment, he pointed toward his wife. As his sons fell for the misdirection, he deftly moistened a pinky finger with his tongue and stuck it in the smaller boy's ear.

"Wet willy!"

"Yuck!" the boy squeaked. He rubbed his ear profusely against his shoulder. Then he wiped it with a napkin. His older brother teased him relentlessly. The young boy scowled in return.

The shop employee placed a lid over the cup and put it in a bag. Leah fished out her wallet and paid with exact change. Her funds were dreadfully low, but she'd receive her mid-month guarantee of five hundred dollars in a week. That is, minus the fifty dollars, one of five installments, she owed Prince Auto for Randall Fenton's seminar.

"Was so nice meeting all of you."

Janet and a couple of kids turned to wave.

"See me in my office if I can help you with anything."

"I sure will."

The real payday, the one with sales commissions, would be in three weeks. She departed through the doors, sweet baby Beka slung over the other hip now.

She had to sell some cars. Quick.

---

1. hat trick
     Slang used to describe selling three cars in one day.
2. cash-in-fist
     Payment in paper currency.
3. money that Momma doesn't need to know about
     An unofficial cash payment that doesn't leave a paper trail.
4. close
     Term to describe the act of convincing a customer to agree to a sales transaction.
5. Momma's boy
     A male customer who needs a parental co-signer to get approved.
6. five-pounder
     A sales transaction with a gross profit of five thousand dollars.
7. over the curb
     A sales transaction that has been completed and the customer has driven the vehicle off the lot.
8. F&I
     An acronym for Finance and Insurance.
9. hammer
     Slang used to describe putting hard pressure on someone.
10. T.O. (turn over)
     Philosophy to never let a customer walk out the door without management intervention.
11. cockroach
     Slang term used by old school salespeople to refer to bad credit customers who they feel are wasting their time.
12. lay down
     Term used to describe a customer who signs on the very first offer.
13. stroke
     Time-wasting shopper.
14. skate
     A term used to describe when a customer is stolen from another salesperson.
15. split

A term used to describe when the commission on a car deal is divided up between two salespeople.

16. weak

A term used to describe a salesperson who cannot close any of his own deals and hasn't sold anything yet.

17. strong

A term used to describe a salesperson who closes a high percentage of car deals.

18. Code four

An attractive female.

19. silver hair

Car buyers who are senior citizens.

20. ducks on the pond

Customers on a car lot.

21. up point

A place where a salesperson stands to wait for the next customer who walks on the lot.

22. *modus operandi*

A well-established method of doing something. (Latin)

23. test drive

Driving of a motor vehicle to determine its drivability or road-worthiness, and general operating state.

24. first pencil

The opening offer from a sales manager, often written onto the four-square worksheet.

FIVE

World of Hurt

M onday morning arrived. Leah dragged herself out of bed before dawn so she could take a hot shower. Within thirty minutes, she was fully dressed for work with her hair pulled back in a ponytail. She gazed at Beka, who was still sound asleep. There was no need to awaken her that early. She pushed the tussle of baby curls aside and gave her forehead a soft kiss.

Ralph and Susie enjoyed their usual morning coffee around the breakfast table. She knew they liked to talk and pray while the girls were still in bed. They were rooted and grounded in love. Leah gave each of them a squeeze and a kiss on the temple.

"Love you, guys."

SHE DROVE into the employee lot and parked next to a white Jeep. It was identical to the one she'd seen the day before, and had a Texas longhorn decal in the rear window. She pressed down the manual lock before she closed the car door, and glanced at the positions of the other three door locks before she took a walk to the front of the main building.

As she passed the used car lot to her left, her heart added a couple of extra beats. There, in an aisle between two rows of Certified Pre-Owned cars, was the young owner of the Wrangler.

Once again, he wore jeans and boots. He walked with the General Manager, who paused beside a used car to puff a few clouds. She admired Mr. Blue Jeans' broad shoulders and slim waist, but his composed hand gestures were what got her attention. He proceeded to make an impassioned plea; Housely overruled at every turn.

She wondered what their disagreement could be about, and why a Prince Auto employee didn't follow dress code.

Inside the showroom, she followed the gaze of a few sales consultants and noticed new surveillance cameras had been installed high up in three corners. She'd guessed the electricians were there for the alarm system. She hadn't been far off. Close enough.

Chuck and Sandra checked out the features of a flashy new car. That reminded Leah they had only two weeks to study the new models and pass sales consultant certifications. Housely had been explicit: when they were not with customers, they were to dedicate every available moment to that task.

Well, that will have to wait.

Leah went over to Moose Stalwart and junior Sales Manager, Erik Harrison, who were in the sales tower[1]. She hoped they wouldn't ask too many questions because she had three prospects from Sunday. If it worked out, she didn't want anyone to copy her methods.

"Morning, guys!"

Erik mumbled something and rubbed his head.

"Wow. You could use some *menudo*[2]."

"How was your Sunday?" Stalwart asked.

"It was good. I have a prospect. Can I get a sales price?"

"Which stock number?"

"P1462A. It wasn't listed on the bonus incentive sheet."

"Here's your copy of the pre-owned price list." Stalwart looked at his computer screen. He didn't say another word.

"Really?"

"Is your customer here right now?"

"No, I met her yesterday."

"Tell her to come in."

"She'll come in for a test drive[3] if she likes our price."

"Tell her she needs to get her butt down here. The Used Car Director will pull several vehicles today."

"Can you do better than seventeen nine ninety-five?"

"That's rock bottom."

"What if she hesitates?"

"Some vehicles will go into the shop for certification, which will bump up their price."

"By how much?"

"About two thousand."

"What does certification mean?"

"They'll be CPOs[4] with an extended warranty. Got it?"

"Yeah, I got it." Leah jotted some notes.

She called all three prospects with the same news about potential certifications that would drive prices up, and she was able to schedule two same-day appointments. The aerobics instructor promised to come by during a break. The lab technician said no one could cover his shift. He wouldn't make it in until that evening.

Leah went to the sales tower and begged Stalwart to delay any action on the two vehicles of interest until the following day. His shoulders vibrated as he quietly laughed to himself and he promised not to do anything rash. Then it dawned on her what he'd done.

Right at that moment, Housely walked into the tower. Stalwart caught him up on what he'd missed.

Her cheeks were on fire.

When they turned toward her, she'd already made haste and was back at her desk. She dialed a phantom phone number and pretended to wait for an answer. Right then, junior Sales Manager Erik jogged over and stopped short when he saw the look on her face.

"What's wrong? You did really good."

"I don't ever want to lie to anybody."

"Yet, you lied to Stalwart."

"How did I lie?"

"You said you had one customer, not two."

"Actually, I have three."

He raised an eyebrow.

She returned the phone to its cradle.

"Look, sometimes you have to massage the truth."

She doodled on her price list.

"Build a sense of urgency. If you don't, customers will walk all over you."

She looked him in the eyes.

"I want to sell a car."

"Okay, I'll help you. That's what I'm here for."

She felt better, but she could see through Erik's façade. He was in pain.

"I know a restaurant that makes really good *menudo*," she offered.

He nodded in surrender and pulled a twenty-dollar bill out of his wallet.

She took the hint.

WHEN SHE RETURNED to the dealership, Erik invited her into the rear corner of the sales tower so they could eat together. Housely and Stalwart were on the other side with a full view of the showroom and the front lots on both sides. Housely wore cushioned headphones.

She looked at the back of his head inquisitively and Erik shrugged.

"He likes to listen to talk radio and live games."

Out of left field, Stalwart asked, "Do you follow baseball?"

Erik let out a moan.

"A little. I don't know any stats, but I enjoy eating a hot dog and watching from the stands. Why?"

"Have you ever been to a Diablos game?"

"Yes, several years ago."

"Your breakfast partner used to play for the Diablos."

Erik's cheekbones were red.

Leah asked Erik a few questions about his background, and he opened up. He was originally from New York, and he'd always dreamed of major league baseball. The Milwaukee Brewers drafted him, and he played outfield positions for a few of their farm teams. He wound up with a couple of seasons with the Diablos before an injury ended his baseball career. By that time, he and a Diablos office employee were serious, so he didn't want to leave. That was when he applied at Prince Auto, and they fast-tracked him to management.

He married his girlfriend last summer, and she was now pregnant.

"Congratulations. That baby is going to bless your socks off."

White-haired Howard stuck his head in. His jaundiced skin accentuated his agitation.

"I need twenty P.O.'s[5]. What time will Gerald be in?"

"He gets here when he gets here," Erik replied.

"Kick rocks," Stalwart ordered.

Howard shut down and retreated.

Her eyes searched Erik's for an explanation.

"He's a cuckold. You want to avoid him at all costs."

"What's a cuckold?"

"Howard and his wife are swingers."

She winced.

"Since she sleeps with other men, he's the definition of a cuckold."

Leah couldn't argue with that logic.

WHEN THEY FINISHED BREAKFAST, she cleaned up the mess and stuffed the trash into a plastic bag. Just before she cleared out, she recalled something and turned around. She hesitated and looked over at the back of Housely's head.

He still wore headphones.

"What did you forget?"

"I meant to ask Housely if I could help his customer."

Erik drew a blank.

"The guy wearing cowboy boots."

Stalwart overheard and turned his head.

"That wasn't a customer. It was Jake."

"Who's Jake?"

"He's our handyman." Stalwart turned back toward his screen.

Erik was more helpful.

"Jake works for Tommy. He does all the repairs at the

mansion and the mountain cabin. The guy must have a set of keys to everything Prince owns. Could be that he's starting a new project here."

"*No problemo*[6]. Going to prepare for my appointment now."

"Alright. Thanks for breakfast."

He rolled his chair away to get a better view of the sales floor.

Leah dashed to her desk for her toothbrush and then went to the ladies' restroom over the service drive to rid herself of onions and other odors that would be offensive to the general public. As she finished up at the sink, Sandra came out of the single stall and struggled with a folded piece of red tulle.

Leah smiled at the mirror.

"Hey. What do you have there?"

"I like to experiment with different outfits."

Leah turned slowly to face the older woman, who wore a black one-piece bathing suit paired with fishnet stockings. She tried not to show alarm.

"That sounds like fun, but don't forget the strict dress code." She took a deep breath and braced for any type of reaction.

Sandra tried to pin the makeshift garland over her left breast.

"Besides, you always look your best in that business suit."

Leah searched and found Sandra's overnight bag in the stall. She pulled out a jacket, pants, and heels.

"Here, let me help you."

Several misfired neurons later, the two fully clothed women walked downstairs together. Sandra stepped into her assigned cubicle and disappeared. Leah tried to look nonchalant as she headed over to the sales tower.

Housely was the first to see her approach. He took off his headphones.

"Something's wrong with Sandra. I think she's unraveling."

"Why don't you start by telling me what happened."

She kept her voice low as she unloaded her testimony. He was silent for much longer than she'd have liked.

"Let me watch her for a little bit."

Leah wasn't satisfied with his response but knew there really wasn't anything else he could do at that point anyway. She nodded, and walked to the reception desk to check out keys to the used car that the aerobics instructor wanted to test drive. A recent rain had spotted the car. She wanted to hose off the dust before her customer arrived.

***

SHE DROVE to the make-ready area where four wash guys detailed vehicles for delivery. A Spanish radio station blared from car speakers. Their faces betrayed surprise as she pulled up beside them and got to work. She borrowed the nozzle, a shammy, and glass cleaner. It didn't have to be perfect but, as she'd seen when she was Mr. Jameson's shadow, a little effort went a long way.

Her first appointment, a thirty-something aerobics instructor, arrived at eleven o'clock. She wore a purple leotard, tights, and legwarmers. There was something regal about her light footsteps and Leah sensed she'd been classically trained in ballet.

A male voice interrupted the music over the intercom.

"Code four[7], main sales floor. Main sales floor, code four."

When he paged code four, sales consultants came out of the woodwork. Some men openly gawked at the Ballet

Dancer's fit physique, while others took several casual glances each. The Managers in the sales tower stood as if their legs had fallen asleep in unison.

Leah shot back warning looks all around. She was thankful her customer wasn't very observant.

After the test drive, the rest of the process was fair and simple. The Ballet Dancer didn't have to trade in her current vehicle; it was fully paid for. Since her Credit Union had already approved her for a loan higher than the dealership's out-the-door price, there really wasn't anything more to do except sign a few documents.

While her customer waited, Leah's nervous hands made copies of an insurance card and driver's license for the deal jacket[8]. Her first sale was about to go on the books.

Stalwart waved her over to the sales tower.

"Our tradition is to cut off a sales consultant's necktie, but you don't wear those. So I cut some cake for you instead."

He pointed to a thick wedge of chocolate frosted yellow cake on a paper plate. There were slices of strawberry and dark red filling. A vertical plastic fork staked Leah's claim.

"Office ladies celebrated March birthdays," Erik explained, and left to assist with another sales consultant's car deal.

She shoveled a forkful into her mouth, and tasted raspberry and chocolate sour cream.

"Yum! How much did I earn?"

"After pack, the store made eighteen hundred on the front end."

She did the calculation in her head.

"Only three hundred sixty bucks?"

"Doesn't qualify for the bonus incentive. Reach for the next stair step."

"Sell five more cars?"

"The percentage increase will be retroactive."

"Gotcha."

Within minutes, Henry the Finance Manager came out of the business office[9]. He led her customer back to his desk and turned to wink at Leah.

"Popped your cherry," he whispered.

His remark ruined her celebratory mood.

---

1. sales tower
    Term used to describe where the sales managers sit when penciling deals.
2. *menudo*
    Traditional Mexican soup made with beef tripe in broth with a red chili pepper base. (Spanish)
3. test drive
    Driving of a motor vehicle to determine its drivability or road-worthiness, and general operating state.
4. CPO (Certified Pre-Owned)
    A used vehicle that has been inspected and refurbished by the dealer.
5. P.O.
    Purchase order.
6. *No problemo*
    No problem. (Spanish)
7. Code four
    An attractive female.
8. deal jacket
    A folder that contains all the information in a customer's transaction.
9. business office
    Slang used to describe the area or office where F&I managers work.

SIX

Finding Favor with Man

er day improved. The lab technician customer arrived a little early with his fiancé, who persuaded him to test drive[1] a new car instead of a used. According to Stalwart's trade appraisal, the customer was woefully upside down[2]. His fiancé owed twelve hundred more than the car was worth. The customer agreed to charge twenty-five hundred to his credit card as down payment, but asked for monthly payments to remain under three fifty. After some mediation with the sales tower[3], they extended the term of his loan to sixty-six months. That put his payment in a range of three forty-nine to three fifty-four, which was within his budget.

Leah took his application. His prime credit rating qualified for a low captive finance rate, which resulted in an even lower payment, but Sales Managers ordered her to feign ignorance. Aldo the Finance Manager would be able to add a point without any friction, or enhance penetration numbers for accidental death and dismemberment insurance.

While they went in to sign paperwork, she went to fill

the gas tank and take off the Monroney sticker. The wash guys had already left for the day. Upon her return, she completed a formal delivery with the aid of a checklist, and asked her customers to return within two weeks to get their free wash and detail.

When everything was done, she hugged them both and wished them happiness. Their wedding day would be in three months. Leah waved goodbye as they drove away.

That put her at two, over the curb[4].

After she parked the trade-in vehicle in the bullpen she came back to the showroom and handed the keys to Stalwart, who placed them in his special metal box. Her second sale was a mini deal so it would pay only one hundred twenty-five dollars.

It was almost 10 p.m. but she felt exhilarated. She wondered if there would be time to grab an up[5] and do a hat trick[6]. There were one, two, three sales consultants who waited for their turn at the up point[7].

"G'night, Leah," Housely said. "We'll close up in fifteen minutes if no one else shows. Come in early tomorrow and be ready to do it all over again."

SHE ALMOST SKIPPED out of there. In the open evening air, two lot attendants parked vehicles by the front door. One of them shouted at her through a driver side window.

"Did you bring your car out yet?"

"No. Why?"

"We're going to lock the gate. Jump in, I'll give you a ride."

She accepted his offer and climbed into the large SUV.

On the way back to the employee parking area, Hal introduced himself. He said he covered new and used cars.

The other lot attendant, Mikey, was responsible for the Truck Center. Every evening, when the main showroom was about to close up, they brought the Managers' vehicles to the portico.

He urged her to never walk in the dark by herself.

She made a mental note to move her car to the front before sunset every day.

Hal's sister, Shelley Mickelson, was the manager of Luxury Imports next door. He said another guy, Timothy, was her lot boy. Leah hadn't visited their showroom yet since they employed a dedicated sales professional and no one else was allowed to sell those cars. Hal mentioned Shelley and Stalwart had lived together for years, then talked excitedly about his big miniature toy car collection. It covered all four walls of his bedroom.

He brought the SUV to a full stop.

"Be careful stepping down. Go on ahead of me and I'll follow you out."

"Thank you, sir. You're a real gentleman." She descended the side steps.

SHE ENTERED the house and heard *The Tonight Show with Jay Leno*. Susie was asleep in front of the TV again, the way she chose to spend most evenings Ralph patrolled the streets on graveyard shift.

Leah peeked into the girls' room. Hannah and Sofia were snug under their princess theme canopies. When she got to her bedroom, she was ecstatic to find Beka happily awake in the crib. She sat her in the middle of the bed and told her all about Mommy's crazy sales day as she changed out of her work clothes.

THE NEXT MORNING, Leah had a sense of foreboding.

She tried but couldn't find Sandra anywhere. She asked Chuck if he'd seen her and his eyes went wide.

"Housely fired her."

"What?"

"A man got past the sales guys on the point. So, I introduced myself. We started to conversate about the new models and then Sandra interrupted."

"Coo-coo-ka-choo," confirmed Chen, a sales consultant with buff arms who overheard.

"She promised to show him a good time."

Leah's mouth dropped open.

"She did. I saw the whole thing."

"Like a hooker with a quota."

"She looked possessed."

Leah worried. "Should I get her things?"

"No need," Chen advised. "Housely made her pack up her desk." He shook his head and walked away.

"Stood by her car and waited until she drove off."

"I wish I had her phone number."

"I wish I'd sold a car. Sandra turned him off and he left."

"I'm sorry that happened. I pray she's okay."

LEAH WAS able to sell a few more units, with the occasional assist from Erik, before her initial end-of-month experience. The long days and late nights that came with the position were nothing compared to that 17-hour-plus marathon day. End-of-month close was when everyone in sales and finance did their last push to get every deal on the books. Prince Auto would pay commissions within two business days.

The biggest hurdles were unfinished deals. Sometimes a customer needed to sign additional paperwork. However, most of the time the deal simply lacked one or two documents for the lending institution (such as proof of residence, or proof of income) or for the DMV[8] (like an insurance binder or unexpired driver's license). As for Leah's deals, they were clean.

Chelsea the finance secretary, who played Lady Luck at the Saturday sales meeting, told her all her deals were with the downstairs ladies for last steps. It didn't matter. Leah was required to remain grounded with her restless teammates until everyone's car deals were complete.

"All hands on deck," the General Manager had said.

The evening grew tedious with the knowledge it would be past midnight before anyone could leave. She got bored of her desk and decided to walk around. As she got up, she picked up a scent similar to what she imagined burnt cornflakes would smell like.

LEAH FELT she understood the dealership ecosystem fairly well. She knew almost every employee in each department, and exactly where to go if she had a question. Her Managers trusted her to be autonomous, as long as she remembered to check in every now and then.

She was on track to make good money; her next paycheck would be more than she'd ever earned for two weeks work. She'd breezed through the new models exam and was an official manufacturer certified sales consultant. If she could keep up, she'd earn a promotion and make a career out of it. Sure, there was still so much for her to learn, and there would be plenty of time for that.

Randall Fenton had insisted they could get ahead in the car business with their integrity intact but many Prince Auto associates fleeced their customers on a daily basis. For instance, Stalwart always estimated the ACV[9] of trade-in vehicles far below the "book value," and sales consultants broke the worrisome news without the bat of an eyelash. They used terms like underwater[10] and upside down as a psychological tactic to elicit cooperation from customers in regards to vehicle price, monthly payment, or down payment.

Leah vowed to herself that she'd never stoop so low, although she might be able to live with a little white lie if it helped move her deal forward. If she ever had the option, she'd want to be oblivious rather than know the unsavory truth. The Managers agreed that was probably her best option anyway because, as they'd repeatedly chastised her, she didn't have a very good poker face.

Housely often preached the personal virtues of a high profit margin. There was a miraculous correlation between a car deal's gross profit and the amount of a down payment. As a result, the craftiest among them persuaded their customers to borrow cash from parents, grandparents, brothers, sisters, cousins, lovers, best friends, neighbors, exes, and even their children's piggy banks. Leah was incredulous when Mo and Abe helped a first-time buyer transport his bandmate's guitars and amps to a pawnshop, unbeknownst to his bandmate, so he could drum up extra cash to buy his dream car.

The Managers encouraged and praised that kind of creativity.

LEAH STOPPED under a lamppost in the used car lot. She couldn't wait for payday to arrive. Her wardrobe was overdue for an update. Around there, Managers looked professional and they set a high bar for everyone else. They dressed for success in designer suits and wore big silver or gold watches.

Every Thursday afternoon like clockwork, the dry cleaner picked up their dirty laundry and delivered freshly pressed shirts and slacks. That very evening, the shoeshine man's van was by the portico. Twenty minutes prior to his arrival, leather shoes started to line up in the hallway that led to the Finance Director's office.

She watched as lot attendants brought Managers' vehicles forward. It seemed everyone drove a late model truck, SUV, or sports car. She'd asked around and found out most were twenty-four or thirty-six-month leases. Her questions prompted the Managers to ask when she planned to trade in her rusty beater. The thought had never crossed her mind, as sentimental as she was about her trusty old friend. That Tempo had transported her safely over 1500 kilometers from *San Patricio*[11], Jalisco, Mexico into El Paso when she was six months pregnant.

When she'd met Joey, the Service Manager, he told her he rebuilt and restored old cars. He showed her several photos of his prized possessions at local auto shows. One of his lowriders made it to the front cover of an auto hobby magazine. It was draped with a scantily clad *chola*[12] in Day of the Dead makeup. Leah said she doubted she'd have much time for any hobbies of her own, at least not for several years. For now, every waking moment away from Prince Auto Plaza was devoted to her little Beka.

He explained that hobby cars weren't only a display of selfish pride; they held the promise of a return-on-investment. Often times he'd win thousands of dollars from an auto show contest, but it was a drop in the bucket compared to the riches he'd gain after a few hours in front of eager buyers or potential sponsors. Joey said Prince Auto paid well enough but he was always hungry for more. Besides, he wasn't the only employee who had a side business. The others just didn't discuss theirs as openly as he did.

She considered that. They practically lived at the dealership six days a week, and many dealership Managers, sales consultants, and service advisors liked to let off steam with their four-by-fours and quads at Red Sands on Sundays. She didn't know how any of them could have time for extracurricular activities. After work during a typical week, she could fend off sleep for maybe one or two hours at the most before she snoozed. On Sundays, she skipped church to prospect for two or three hours. Counting all the hours she was awake and away from the dealership, she might be able to eke out twenty-four hours per week—but that meant zero time for Beka or anyone else.

The thought of off-roading did sound like fun. She wondered if mothers and small children were welcomed on those excursions to the sandbox. From the way the men talked, their expensive toys were in a constant cycle of abuse and repair. She envied their disposable income.

Housely and Roberto, the Body Shop Manager, didn't like to roll around in the dirt so they rode Harleys. Every other year, the *compadres*[13] took a road trip to the Rocky Mountain Oyster Festival. The event was renowned for its debauchery and drunkenness so, if they didn't post bail, it was considered a wasted weekend. Some salesmen called it The Testicle Festival and she envisioned gay Hell's Angels entangled in a crude game of Twister. When she asked Erik what they'd meant, he informed her that it was a food festival centered on a delicacy: bovine testis, flattened and fried to perfection. She grimaced, but was inwardly relieved she'd never have to picture Housely and Roberto in bottomless riding chaps again.

AFTER LEAH HAD WORKED THERE for a few weeks, car salesmen morphed into caricatures before her very eyes. For instance, the puffy-chested Chihuahuas (Tito, Mario, and Rogelio) worked at the new truck building and always traveled as a pack. Each man was short and stout to begin with, and they assumed a wide, defensive stance identical to the posture she learned in self-defense class. Their smack talk sounded like three high-pitched dogs' "yap-yap-yap" and yelps.

Two loudmouthed bulldogs (Ben and Chen) were weightlifters in tailor-made shirts. They constantly compared their biceps and pecs to each other and the next guy. Each claimed to be on a diet of hard-boiled eggs or canned tuna, in addition to multiple daily protein milkshakes. Co-workers seemed to admire the discipline but nevertheless ate tempting carbs and saturated fats in front of them. Leah didn't want to point out the lost battleground around the bulldogs' beer-bloated midsections. It might bruise their egos and she hadn't known the Marine officer, or the rehabilitated felon, long enough to make that kind of crack.

Then there were identical twin brothers nicknamed The Camel Jockeys, which made Leah picture a camel in a jockey uniform. Mr. Jameson told her it meant they were Persians. He said he didn't know what their country of origin was, nor did he care. Both Mo and Abe were new car sales consultants and their aunt was married to Gerald, the Finance Director. Some of the salesmen also liked to call Gerald's young nephews House Mice behind their backs, especially when Housely or Stalwart fed referral customers to them.

The brothers seemed to be on a part-time schedule, which was unheard of in the car business, and they were never required to take an up from the lot. No one dared to ask questions.

Leah knew nepotism could be harmful to the workplace, but she figured that was just the way things worked. People were loyal to their own people. It was basic survival instinct to construct a perpetual circle of protection around one's tribe. She felt she'd also favor family members and close friends if it were in her power to do so.

Mr. Jameson also informed Leah that Betty the Comptroller was Stalwart's ex-wife and also Housely's sister. That surprised her, because she didn't think the General Manager looked related to High-Bangs Betty with the heavy eyeliner. Mr. Jameson further revealed that Housely had an on-again, off-again, dalliance with Melanie the Advertising Manager. According to him, Melanie was reportedly volatile but it was understandable because Housely was reputed for being a lady's man.

Through a puff of smoke that was bitter to Leah's taste buds, Mr. Jameson continued to school her about close-knit personal relationships of which she knew naught. Although he didn't mention the relationship between Stalwart and Shelley, manager of Luxury Imports, he said there were unbreakable bonds between Stalwart, Gerald, Robert, and Housely. They'd worked together at another dealership for many years. He viewed their relatively short stint at Prince Auto Plaza as incomparable to his own twenty-plus years with the company.

In 1995, after Prince Auto's longtime Comptroller

passed away, High-Bangs Betty stepped out of an eighties time machine and into the role of financial director. She'd persuaded Tommy to permit an undercover financial investigation into his sales team. Subsequently, their last General Manager died an untimely and suspicious death and Housely was asked to commandeer the ship. He swiftly replaced almost every dealership Manager with a member of his hand-picked crew.

It was a sudden, hostile takeover.

Mr. Jameson recommended to Leah that she steer clear of workplace romance. He stubbed out the embers and removed his sunglasses.

"Keep it professional, especially with those Managers."

The senior sales pro grabbed the next up before she could respond.

The sting of his insinuation was sobering.

---

1. test drive
    Driving of a motor vehicle to determine its drivability or roadworthiness, and general operating state.
2. upside down
    A term to describe the condition of owing more than a vehicle's worth.
3. sales tower
    Term used to describe where the sales managers sit when penciling deals.
4. over the curb
    A sales transaction that has been completed and the customer has driven the vehicle off the lot.
5. up
    A customer who walks on the lot.
6. hat trick
    Slang used to describe selling three cars in one day.
7. up point
    A place where a salesperson stands to wait for the next customer who walks on the lot.
8. DMV
    Department of Motor Vehicles.

9. ACV (Actual Cash Value)

    Wholesale value assigned to a vehicle at trade-in, based on guides and estimated cost of reconditioning.

10. underwater

    A term to describe the condition of owing more than a vehicle's worth.

11. *San Patricio*

    A village in Jalisco, Mexico. Literally, "Saint Patrick." (Spanish)

12. *chola*

    A young woman belonging to a Mexican American subculture commonly associated with street gangs. (Spanish)

13. *compadres*

    A traditional term to describe mutual reverence and friendship, often between a child's parent and godparent. (Spanish)

SEVEN

What Do Women Want

Leah was astonished the Sales and Finance Managers worked fourteen hour days and rarely left for anything, even a meal. If they wanted breakfast, lunch, or dinner, they called a restaurant and sent a lot attendant or a sales consultant to fetch the order. "I buy, you fly" was a deal they made to compensate sales consultants with a meal for the time they spent away from the sales floor.

She soon discovered it wasn't unusual for a group of Managers to drop a thousand dollars cash on a special order of sushi after a productive sales week. The sushi restaurant owner insisted on personal delivery via a temperature-controlled vehicle which turned out to be his wife's white minivan. Dealership Managers never objected because no one in their right mind wanted to eat bad raw fish and get poisoned.

However, there were plenty of other reasons not to send a sales consultant for the sushi order but those never occurred to Leah until Erik told her about them.

Firstly, the sushi man valued their repeat business, and

the Sales Managers knew it. Every time he came by, they showed him a shiny new vehicle they knew his wife wouldn't approve. As a result, every two or three months, he sent them a primed referral out of a sense of obligation. When the referral purchased a Prince Auto vehicle, Managers kept the sushi man's one hundred dollar bird-dog[1] fee for themselves and applied it to their next sushi order.

Erik said another reason Managers wouldn't send sales consultants for the sushi order, even someone who was star-certified in food safety standards, was the simple fact they didn't trust them. They suspected the designated driver would take off with the cash, the sushi order, or both. Apparently, there was a legendary salesman who pulled off that exact stunt, but for far less. His Manager handed him a twenty-dollar bill to pick up a happy hour special: a sack of cheeseburgers and fries. The young salesman took off like he'd made bail and never returned.

A few days later, a police detective notified Prince Auto their employee had held up a fast food restaurant. The salesman pistol-whipped a learning disabled crewmember, stole cash from the register, and absconded with a sack of burgers and fries.

Leah punched Erik's arm.

He swore on his grandmother's grave it was true but she was skeptical.

Another celebratory order for the Managers was a large foil pan of appetizers from the Mediterranean restaurant. It required twenty-four hours' notice to prepare: lamb and rice stuffed grape leaves with plain yogurt dip. The Managers were addicted to it.

Frank, the Truck Manager, ordered another to share with his kids on Sunday. According to his version of events, he'd won full custody of two daughters after his nasty divorce. His wife initiated the separation but, when he paid a small fortune to an attorney and a private investigator, he was able to provide the court with evidence of his wife's illicit drug abuse and sex addiction. Now his elderly parents cared for the girls six days a week. Their mother had supervised visitation every other Saturday.

They would turn four in a few months.

Finance Director Gerald Allen walked with a waddle and was the poster boy for gastric bypass surgery. Leah was certain a large hula hoop couldn't pass over his tremendous girth. Once, when she glanced at his fine leather belt, she thought she heard a moo from the slaughtered red heifer.

She didn't understand why anyone would want to wear his pants cinched so painfully high, until she came to terms with the fact it was an attempt to conceal excess flab. Theoretically, if he let his pants hug his hips below the stomach, as many other men did, he'd need to construct a retaining wall for those loose bags of flesh below his waist-line. However, even if a compression girdle in his size existed, he'd still have the silhouette of a caramel apple on a stick. There was nothing he could do to drastically alter his appearance, and any major effort would severely restrict blood circulation. By pulling his pants up high, at least it provided a curtain of sorts to shield unsightly jiggly parts from view and his body parts could have some space to breathe.

Gerald's usual order was a plain fast food burger with ketchup only. The first time he sent her out for one, she politely asked if he'd like to add fries, onion rings, soda, or a milkshake. He became irate. The experience reminded her of a spoiled pre-pubescent she'd babysat once upon a time.

As the boy requested, she cooked a made-to-order hamburger without anything on it besides two pieces of bread, meat, and ketchup. The problem began when she made herself one and added a slice of American cheese. He laid down on his back and kicked in circles like a stuck tortoise until he peed his pants. His ex-beauty queen mother didn't return from her social function until a stranger's car dropped her off in front of the house at 4 a.m. She'd smelled of cheap sex and wine.

Leah gagged the first time she saw Gerald eat fried chicken. He peeled off the flavorful skins, greedily slurped them up, and hardly remembered to chew before he swallowed. After he discarded the good meat with the bones, he tossed everything into the trashcan by his desk, and languidly licked the oily residue off his paws. Then he lit an apple scented candle and got back on the phone to hammer[2] the banks some more.

That day she had a vision of the inside of his chest, behind his ribcage and beneath the lungs. A lifetime of trans fats weighed down his heart. As the vital muscular organ struggled and fought for space, its plaque-filled arteries worked overtime to pump life-sustaining resources to his arms, legs, and brain. It would fail miserably.

SHE DIDN'T REACH the top of the leaderboard and win the prestigious Salesperson of the Month plaque, because that honor went to "Top Dog" Reverend Bobby Dean, but she was very happy with the nice check she received on payday. Susie was pleasantly surprised when Leah paid her two hundred dollars and promised it would become a regular occurrence.

When a skinny salesman named Carlos said he wanted to show Leah an affordable Mexican eatery nearby, she remembered Mr. Jameson's warning about fraternization and declined his offer. Carlos promised there were no strings attached, and she'd enjoy the mouthwatering *tortas*[3]. Since she wasn't physically attracted to him, she agreed to go.

They checked out early for dinner on a slow afternoon, with plans to return within the hour. He drove an old hooptie but she didn't mind. When he pulled into the entrance, he parked far away by the very edge of the vacant lot next door. She was thankful her comfortable flip-flops were in her bag.

Carlos told her he'd worked at Prince Auto for three years, and he had a side hustle as Prince Auto's in-house loan shark. It was a prolific venture because most sales consultants lacked a budget and self-discipline. Several first-time credit applicants got into trouble simply because they lived paycheck to paycheck. A few of his repeat clients fell into arrears with child support payments or had other legal issues. Some frequented tribal casinos after work.

He said his terms were not unreasonable. In the event the debtors couldn't make a minimum payment, they could always come to him for a possible extension. However, after a short grace period passed, the total amount was due. Leah pictured cracked kneecaps and wanted to know how he enforced repayment of the loans. He explained that he made sales consultants sign a secured promissory note. Prince Auto's payroll department always had his back. Payments were deducted from the debtor's next paycheck.

Carlos and Leah both ordered the same platter and she was pleased with how tasty the meaty *tortas* turned out. He asked if she planned to eat the whole thing. She laughed at the sarcasm but, when he followed up with a disparaging remark about her bulge, she knew he was serious. Her post-pregnancy belly still had some jiggle and she was more than a little self-conscious about it.

When the server brought the check, Carlos insisted that he pay for all of it. Then he wanted to leave before Leah finished her seasoned fries. She decided against asking for a to-go box.

When they got outside, a dry breeze blew through the busy traffic sounds and the sky had dimmed to azure. They arrived at his car, and Carlos opened her door first before he conveyed a half-hearted apology. He explained it had been a rough week. Something about difficulties with his parents. He walked around to the driver side and got in.

She forgave him but she kept her mental notes.

He tried to turn the conversation around.

"I'm impressed with how quickly you picked up sales."

"Really?"

"If you ever need me, let me know."

"I know why you brought me here."

"You do?"

"To pitch your high-interest payday loans."

They laughed at that and he wagged his finger at her. He started the engine and lowered his seat all the way back.

"Ugh, I'm so bloated. Look at how fat I am." He was razor thin.

"Shut up."

"No, I mean it. I can't get a breath. Turn up the AC."

She searched for the knob and turned it clockwise.

"How's that feel?"

"That's good. Hey, why don't you lower your seat?"

She gave him the side-eye.

"Look at the stars for a few minutes. I'll show you Orion." He indicated the sunroof above their heads.

"Okay, I will, but I know ten ways to kill a man with the heel of my shoe."

Carlos led into a comfortable, albeit geeky, explanation of gassy giants and supernovas. They looked up through the tilted glass and out the windshield. Leah listened with wonder about the immense galaxy. After a minute, she felt his gaze wander over her. She was afraid to look in his direction and remained in the center of her seat.

"Heavenly Father," she filled the awful silence. "You never cease to amaze me."

"Jee-zus. You're one of those?"

He launched his seat forward and sat upright.

There you are.

"I'm one of those what?"

"We really should be getting back."

He put his car into reverse as she sat up and merrily clicked her seatbelt.

"Next time, it's my treat."

———

STALWART TOLD Leah to grab the keys to a specific stock number. He explained that Tommy Prince would be down in about fifteen minutes. She was to drive him to Doña Ana County regional airport. Stalwart commanded her to blast the AC to cool the interior and, while she was at it, check the tire pressure and make sure there was a sufficient gas for a round trip. He seemed jittery as if it were her first trip around the block.

She rolled her eyes and went off to find the car in the used car lot. It turned out to be a recently washed red convertible with leather seats. Within ten minutes, she pulled the clean-smelling car into the portico and waited.

Their dealer principal came downstairs right on time.

He wore slacks and a salmon golf shirt that exposed tan arms. His hair wasn't in the typical slicked back style, so his black mane moved naturally.

She waved.

He got into the front seat and placed his leather satchel on the floorboard. She immediately discerned a subtle blend of salty sea spray, wet earth, and sage. Instantly, she felt an unmistakable undercurrent and thought she could hear the distant surf. His scent made her crave an evening dip in the Pacific.

"What's your name?"

"Leah Owers, I'm one of the new hires."

"Tommy Prince. Call me Tommy."

She carefully put the car into gear.

Several rubberneckers and smokers idled and tracked her every move. In a flicker, darkness eclipsed Tommy's eyes. The power window rolled down and he thundered at them to find something better to do. It caused an immediate stir. They broke off their stares and dispersed.

The window rolled up and he returned to his usual, public-facing disposition. He wanted to know about Leah's first few weeks and how she liked it there so far. She only had positive things to report. Then she learned a little about him: He owned a personal jet, and employed a pilot and a steward. Old friends in California owned a vineyard and they'd invited him to visit. He'd be away for a week.

She inquired about his hobbies and discovered he was a humanitarian. He dedicated spare time to the underprivileged. He served on several boards, and his primary charitable cause was breast cancer research. When she asked how he got his start in the car business, he delved into the proud family heritage.

Tommy was third generation Prince automotive royalty. His immigrant grandfather, Thomas Prince I, had finagled his way into majority ownership of a franchise in the early part of the century. Their initial dealership was located in downtown El Paso. The historic building was now a popular stop on the acclaimed Ghost Tour. Paranormal investigation groups flocked to it.

In recent years, after Grandpa Prince passed, reporters and authors requested interviews with the family. They had questions regarding backdoor deals with mobsters and blackmail of city and county officials. Tommy refused any such meetings. He was adamant Grandpa was a good man, a visionary, who happened to have a keen survival instinct and an indomitable spirit.

Tommy's only child, Jimmy, played on a high school soccer team. He said his son was excited to get his driver's license. Jimmy's mother, Mara Elena, was a stunner. Tommy knew he had to have her as soon as he saw her at a party in the eighties. She wore a white satin gown. A famous Hollywood producer stood beside her.

He spoke of her in the past tense.

"Did something happen to your wife?"

"She's been in a vegetative state for several months."

"Oh, I'm so sorry."

She kept her eyes on the road ahead and remembered a newspaper photo of Mara Elena Prince at a Christmas gala. If only she'd read the article, she might know more about her condition.

"It was her prescription sleep medicine. One of the Woman's Club members talked to the press and said it was a cry for help. Her so-called friend embarrassed our family. I'll never forgive her for that."

She drove over railroad tracks on to Country Club Road. Soon they crossed over the Texas-New Mexico border.

"I knew Mara better than anyone, and she was very

happy. She had everything a woman could want. Most people were envious."

The radio's volume was low, so they could hear the steady road noise pass under the floorboard. As they approached the airfield, he helped her navigate around it until they reached the correct hangar.

"Before I go, I want you to tell me one thing I can do to improve Prince Auto Plaza for our valued clients."

Leah put the car into park and looked him in the eyes.

"Fix those restrooms."

She explained the ladies' room in the main building, over the service drive, was antiquated and needed an update to modern standards. It didn't even have a table to change a baby's diaper. She told him about a mother who had no option but to spread paper towels on the bathroom floor. There was only one stall in there, and three total female stalls on the corner lot. The small rectangular mirror, over a tiny counter with a single sink, was insufficient if there were more than one woman in the room. And so on.

He listened closely and agreed the building had been designed by men and for men. Back then, there were far fewer female employees or female visitors. One hundred percent of their main clientele used to be male. If a female was ever involved in a transaction, she was someone ancillary to the deal like a wife, fiancé, or daughter. He relayed new statistics he'd heard at a recent automotive dealer conference: Approximately half of all shoppers and buyers were women, and a female decision maker influenced most sales outcomes.

"That sounds right. Lines up with my experience."

Tommy considered the possible return on his investment. He looked out the windshield.

"I'll think it over. See you in a week or two."

He picked up his satchel and exited the car.

She waited as he disappeared behind a partition. A yell of victory rose in her throat, but she held on until she was back on the main road.

Then she let loose.

---

1. bird-dog
   A fee paid for a customer referral.
2. hammer
   Slang used to describe putting hard pressure on someone.
3. *tortas*
   Mexican sandwiches. (Spanish)

EIGHT

The Golden Rule

I t was lunchtime. Leah carefully drove the diesel one-ton dually between two lanes of assorted vehicles near the make-ready area. She parked it, applied the parking brake, and shut off the engine. Her customer wanted to enjoy his new truck as much as possible before he reported for his next shift at the fire station. She hoped her plan would work. She clutched the keys, an Ardovino's pizza box, and a chilled six-pack of cokes, and daintily stepped out of the cab. She placed both feet on the running board and carefully stepped down to the asphalt.

Joyful Mexican *ranchera*[1] music echoed off the concrete walls of the single-level parking garage. She'd been back there several times before, every time she sold a vehicle that needed a detail. It was the same process every time: she'd hand over the keys to Jesús, the lead washman with salt-and-pepper hair, and he'd hang them on the pegboard in order of priority.

Stalwart told her the best practice was to set customer expectations for next-day delivery, and to bring the vehicle to make-ready four or five hours in advance. The wash guys were busy most mornings and afternoons, especially on Saturday, so sales consultants would usually schedule their customers' deliveries in the evening or early the following weekday. Same day delivery was possible only on very slow sales days, Stalwart said.

She looked around and estimated twenty vehicles were ahead of her.

One of the younger men yelled something in Spanish and Jesús came out of a blue compact car. She handed over the food gift but held back the truck keys. He gave her an inquisitive look. She wasn't fully bilingual but she could converse in some classroom Spanish. She decided at the last second not to sound stupid in front of the native speaker.

"This is for you and your guys."

Jesús made an unusual utterance that sounded like appreciation, and shouted for the others to come over. He opened the box and offered each of them a slice of combo pizza topped with *jalapeño*[2]. Before he served himself, he took the truck keys from her and pointed to the dually to make sure it was the correct vehicle.

"Yes. What time will it be ready?"

"*A la una y media*[3]." That was less than two hours away.

She gave him a brilliant smile and returned to the showroom. She relayed the good news to her Firefighter and his buddy. Since he was finished with finance, he decided to try the *tortas*[4] at the Mexican restaurant she recommended. He said he'd be back by 2 p.m. at the latest.

As they walked out, Chuck came over reluctantly and told her she'd been skated[5]. A little earlier, he overheard a sales consultant approach customers who asked for Leah by name. They must have been her two o'clock appointment, but they'd arrived earlier than previously agreed. She was busy with the Firefighter at the time.

Yermo lied, said she wasn't in, and took over from there.

Now they were on a test drive[6].

"I wish I'd upped them myself," Chuck apologized. "I wouldn't expect a split[7] deal, and I know you'd do the same for me."

She nodded, and became increasingly indignant with each second that passed.

It was the only time she'd been skated, and it felt like a betrayal. She'd have to put her foot down now or Yermo, or someone else, would do it again. She appealed to the General Manager, but he had no compassion.

"You need to control your customers better."

"But they asked for me!"

"Watch your tone," he growled.

Leah checked herself.

"Other than lie to them, the only thing he has done is go for a test drive. That doesn't deserve half a car deal."

"Yermo is adept at fact-finding and holding gross. You don't want to interrupt the momentum he's been building this entire time."

"For crying out loud, he should have told someone to page me."

His eyes flickered red.

Leah was disheartened. She could already tell it was futile to present any more facts. Housely was irredeemably biased.

She looked away.

A wolf dared to pluck one of her sheep from the fold. A fluffy ewe that would have produced wool and lanolin for many seasons, or birthed enough lambs to create a separate flock. All that remained was a half-consumed carcass. The apex predator's ravenous impulses demanded raw flesh. His thick cranium didn't give a thought toward the female sales rep he'd just skated. If she wanted to be a shrewd shepherdess, she must learn to protect her sheep. She alone was responsible for what happened to them.

"Take the easy half-deal. Watch him work. You might learn something."

She felt Housely's last comment like a backhand to the face. He put his headphones on and looked at his computer monitor. The discussion was over.

Her cheeks flushed red hot.

Chuck dodged out of her way as she made a hasty retreat to the restroom.

She passed the fish aquarium and grumbled like a petulant child.

"Watch him work. You might learn something. I'd rather jump off a cliff."

"Excuse me. Ma'am?"

"Huh?" She snapped to attention and spun around to search for the source.

It was one of the service porters. Next to him was a weatherworn man in overalls and dusty boots, who clutched a straw hat to his chest.

"This gentleman asked to see our new trucks."

"Of course. Happy to help."

THE OLD FARMER had been on I-10 East when his '86 pickup made an odd noise. He was on a return trip and lived about three and a half hours southeast of El Paso. He decided to stop at the nearest franchise dealership. A gas station attendant gave him directions to Prince Auto Plaza. Unfortunately, their service department was booked for the next forty-eight hours, but he wasn't upset. He just wanted to get the pickup towed and he'd tinker with it at his house.

In the meanwhile, he required a new work truck that was operational. He wanted to see trucks without the bells and whistles. Preferred a tan color. Small V8 was fine. Automatic and AC. Manual locks and windows. She asked if a trailer-tow package, or tinted windows were important to him. He thought about those but decided against either option.

The Truck Center was a portable building with a ramp that led to the door. As the Farmer stayed outside to look around some more, Leah excused herself to retrieve keys to a single cab. It perfectly suited her customer's wants and needs.

Frank, the Truck Sales Manager, and the three Chihuahuas, lounged around and ate caramel popcorn while they waited for an "up." The rules were a little lax on that side of the corner lot. She perused the keys in the cabinet next to Frank's desk.

"Hi, guys."

"Another one? Look at you! What's the stock number?"

"T2398." She removed the key.

Frank searched through his list.

"That one qualifies for the two hundred fifty dollar aged unit bonus."

She did the math in her head.

"Three hundred seventy-five bucks, even if it's a mini?"

"You got it. My loaner is blocking it in. I'll get Mikey." He paged the lot attendant.

"I really need this deal. Promise me you'll do everything in your power?"

"Always." He grabbed a set of keys from the center desk drawer.

Mikey stumbled in. Frank tossed the keys to him.

"Aaaggh!"

The Chihuahuas rolled with laughter.

Mikey retrieved the keys from the tile floor, embarrassed.

"Move my loaner to the other side of the building."

Mikey darted out the door.

Leah was confused.

"What just happened here?"

"He has a glass eye. Poor hand-eye coordination."

She walked quickly to the door, uncomfortable with his cruel idea of a joke.

"I heard Yermo put on his roller skates," Tito piped up.

"Yeah."

She stepped out into the heat.

My, how quickly these men spread gossip.

---

1. *ranchera*

    Songs that originated on the ranches and countryside of rural Mexico. (Spanish)

2. *jalapeño*

    A very hot, green chili pepper used in Mexican-style cooking. (Spanish)

3. *A la una y media*

    At 1:30. (Spanish)

4. *tortas*

    Mexican sandwiches. (Spanish)

5. skate

    A term used to describe when a customer is stolen from another salesperson.

6. test drive

    Driving of a motor vehicle to determine its drivability or road-worthiness, and general operating state.

7. split

    A term used to describe when the commission on a car deal is divided up between two salespeople.

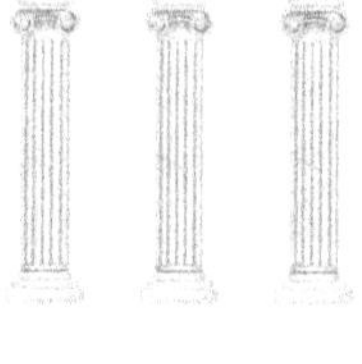

NINE

Hat Trick

Leah fired on all cylinders that afternoon and balanced multiple customer appointments. When she and the Farmer returned from the test drive[1], she sat him in the main showroom because he wanted to call his bank to arrange the wire transfer. She asked Erik for an assist because her customer would need a P.O.[2] with the out-the-door price. Then she excused herself to get her other customer's truck out of make-ready before he returned from lunch.

She drove it to the gas station and filled its large tank with diesel. By the time she drove back to the lot, the Firefighter and his buddy were on the portico. She sat them in the truck while she went to get the owner's manual and the extra set of keys.

She was about to check on the Farmer, but Erik said he was taken care of. He was now in Henry's office where he'd be asked to sign vehicle registration documents. He'd agreed to pay full MSRP[3] minus applicable factory rebates plus tax, title, and license, as long as the service department would arrange for a free tow. The dealership would deduct the cost of the tow job from the deal's ample gross.

When Leah stopped at Yermo's desk, she clapped the fastidiously groomed man on the back and introduced herself to her stolen customers. She apologized for the apparent miscommunication earlier and they were very gracious about it. Since there were two partially-filled credit applications on the desk, she congratulated their decision to purchase from Prince Auto Plaza. The salesman's stunned face gave a thin smile to her flawless performance.

She glanced at the sales tower[4].

The eyes of Housely, Stalwart, and Erik were on her.

She went outside to complete an abbreviated delivery process because the Firefighter was ready to go. He affixed a bumper sticker with the image of a mallard duck in flight. It read Keep Honking, I'm Reloading. She tried not to snort but couldn't help it. His buddy didn't say much but he smiled warmly. Before her customer left, he signed a delivery checklist to indicate he was pleased with everything.

She went back inside to retrieve the Farmer's new floor mats, owner's manual, and extra set of keys. While she waited for him to come out of finance, Erik handed her a bottle of spring water and ordered her to drink it. He said sunshine and non-stop activity dehydrated athletes and sales consultants alike, and she wouldn't faint on his watch. She did as she was told and couldn't remember the last time cool refreshment felt so good.

When the Farmer emerged, she drove him back to make-ready. She had to find a blade to take off the Monroney sticker. He said the truck was as clean as it would ever be, so there was no need to try for more.

Mindful of the time of day, he said he wanted to get back by sunset.

Since she knew from the test drive he was quick witted and possessed a laugh-out-loud sense of humor, she proceeded with the delivery process in an officious and ostentatious manner.

Expressionless, she checked off each item with a sweep of her pen. As he signed the document, she informed him in a royal British accent he was obliged to telephone her when he ultimately disembarked, or he'd unsettle her feminine nerves. He gave his word as both a gentleman and a countryman, whatever that meant.

After their theatrics, they doubled over with laughter despite themselves, and exchanged phone numbers. She felt a deep sense of satisfaction as he drove off the lot and merged into city traffic.

LEAH HADN'T VISITED the restroom in hours. She didn't want to go all the way upstairs just to be disappointed to find the single stall was occupied, so she went down a few short steps to ask the office ladies if she could use theirs. She knocked on their Dutch door. The clerk who came over was not used to visitors but she let Leah in when she read her nametag. Within sixty seconds, Leah went from gratefulness to total relief.

She almost didn't make it in time.

When she came out, Jan the Office Manager waited for her. Several worker bees looked on but remained in their cubicles.

"Two bucks for the ladies' lottery pool. If we get a winner, we split the jackpot."

Leah reached into her pocket for the cash and tossed it in.

"Heard the new ad drew in a swarm today."

"Which one? My customers didn't mention it."

"No, the job ad," corrected the title clerk. She looked a lot like President Clinton's famous intern. "For female sales consultants."

"Oh! The more the merrier."

Jan and the title clerk looked at Leah as if antennas poked out of her green head.

A much younger clerk stifled a giggle.

"Betty said they're drawing up plans for bathroom renovations."

"Awesome."

"I hope they put in one of those new diaper changing trays," said the title clerk.

"Yeah, and a cabinet," Leah suggested. "For now, everything is in the large bottom drawer of my desk on the left side. Feel free to borrow whatever you need. I'm fully stocked."

"Aww, that's so nice!" the younger clerk gushed.

"Plus, I have a chocolate stash. But my rule is you have to stay and talk to me for a couple minutes."

"Is that right?" Jan questioned. She squinted over her glasses.

Leah didn't flinch.

"I'm fine with you talking to my employees while they're on a break, but I don't want to hear Housely complain. You understand?"

Leah gave a nod.

"In the meanwhile, I'll see about installing a lock on your desk."

"That'd be great."

"LEAH OWERS, LINE ONE."

The voice didn't sound like 41-year-old Valerie, the main receptionist. She looked over at the reception desk. A young natural redhead sat next to a younger Latina trainee with braces. They both smiled and waved.

She looked out the wall of windows on the way to her desk. Wind gusts had picked up speed, so dry leaves and sand made a scraping sound as they brushed against the glass. Pale orange rays reminded her it was time to move the car forward. She lifted the receiver to her ear and pressed the blinking button.

"Thank you for calling Prince Auto Plaza, where we're having the sale of a lifetime. This is Leah, how may I assist you?"

"You can start by cutting the crap." Hearty laughter.

"Oh! You got me."

She was relieved the Farmer had made it safely to his destination. From their previous conversation, he lived in the countryside and his wife had passed.

"Sweet, Miss Leah. The good life is about more than lots of money. Don't get me wrong; I'm thankful you were put in my path today. I thought about it the whole time I was driving back. I said, 'LORD, I never had so wonderful an experience buying a truck. Bless dear Miss Leah and her baby girl.'"

Her heart glowed with appreciation.

"I tell you what, you made it easy as ordering flapjacks at the diner. By the way, have you ever worked as a waitress?"

"Yes sir, I have. The next time you come to El Paso, look me up. I'll treat you to a good Mexican meal."

"You got yourself a deal, young lady. I don't turn down free food."

She laughed.

"I'll make sure to wear bigger overalls, so we can get your money's worth." He roared.

AFTER SHE MOVED the car forward, she went to Erik in the sales tower to express her appreciation and to see if he needed anything. He set aside a section of newspaper and yawned.

"You want some coffee?"

"Nah."

He looked over at Housely, Stalwart, and a female who wore a black miniskirt that showed off her pretty legs. They deliberated around a small table on the sales floor. The other tables were occupied by customers and salesmen with crimson smirks.

Leah tried to sound copacetic about the new hottie as she glanced at the newspaper in front of Erik.

"One of the job applicants?"

"No. They were out of here by noon. She's the ad rep."

"Melanie?"

"No! Not the Advertising Manager." He laughed and pulled out a chair for her. "She's our advertising representative, for a national magazine that publishes vehicle listings."

"Okay. Tell me more."

"Last time she was here, she brought her modeling portfolio. She was totally nude in some of the photographs."

Leah eyes rolled into the back of her head.

"Not about the ad rep. The listings."

Erik sat up straight.

"Every year Housely and Melanie like to look through the advertising expenses and cut the fat. Melanie takes care of TV and radio, and Housely takes care of print."

"I see. Continue."

"Watch this. In a minute, Housely will show the ad rep some listings with the wrong price or other flaws. Then he'll threaten to cancel the account."

"Tough customer. Wouldn't want to be in her shoes."

"She's expecting it. I'll bet you she has a partial refund check in her purse."

"Seriously?"

"Serious as a heart attack. The magazine sends a new girl every twelve to eighteen months to keep it interesting, but she knows how to do this dance."

Bulldog Chen came up to the sales tower. Skinny Carlos trailed behind him.

"Boss, me and my loan shark friend are going to check what's on the menu at Hooters."

"Make sure you're back in an hour."

Leah made an ugly face. Chuck had confided in her that when a man at Prince Auto said, "check what's on the menu at Hooters," it was code for one of two things: the man was either off to a strip club, or to a questionable massage parlor. Both activities frequently involved something commonly referred to as a "happy ending."

Chen turned to Leah with delirious delight.

"Sucky-sucky!"

A silver hair[5] picked that exact moment to shuffle past. The outburst scared the woman. She defiantly raised her cane.

"It's an affliction," Carlos apologized to her. He used

both hands to push Chen's bulky frame through the open doorway.

The junior Sales Manager was focused on Leah's face.

She glanced at him, then looked away.

"You weren't supposed to understand what Chen said. I'm so sorry."

"You don't have to apologize."

"Aren't you and Carlos—?"

"Are me and Carlos what?" She furrowed her eyebrows.

"Never mind."

Stalwart and Housely wrapped up their Come-To-Jesus meeting with the ad rep and re-entered the sales tower.

"Sales consultants aren't supposed to be in the tower," Housely announced to no one in particular. He placed a stack of magazines and papers on the U-shaped wrap-around desk. "But hold your horses."

He turned toward the hottie who had walked up to the sales tower.

"See you later," she said. He gave her a sly grin.

Housely returned his attention to Leah and ceremoniously pulled a hundred dollar bill out of his wallet.

"For your hat trick[6]."

Erik sat back with a satisfied look.

"Well done," Stalwart appraised.

It slowly occurred to her. Being skated[7] by Yermo had thrown off her count. That deal, plus the Firefighter, and the Farmer made three fresh deals in one day.

She squealed.

"Thank you, God!"

Housely exhaled. "I need to smoke." He left the sales tower[8]. Stalwart and Erik followed.

"Hey, can I borrow your newspaper?"

Erik tossed up his hand in acknowledgement.

She was curious about the employment ad. She didn't know which section it would be in, so she gathered all she could find. She left Stalwart's crossword puzzle untouched and ignored Erik's sports section. Her eyes continued to search until they landed on Housely's stack of papers.

There were two checks, one over the other. The magazine's name and address were in bold print, and the top check was payable to Prince Auto Imports for four thousand five hundred dollars. She almost whistled but held back. Her finger slid it aside so she could read the check underneath. It was from the same company, payable to Prince Used Cars. Six thousand dollars. A combined advertising refund of more than ten thousand dollars. Erik had been right.

She put the check back in its original position.

"Leah Owers," paged a female voice.

She jumped.

"Customer on line two." The Redhead smiled and held up two fingers to remind her.

Leah turned and tripped over the General Manager's heavy briefcase. Laughter echoed throughout the showroom and stung almost as much as the scrape on her shin. Apparently, evening at the Greek improv was a hit.

She hadn't meant to be so conspicuous.

---

1. test drive
     Driving of a motor vehicle to determine its drivability or roadworthiness, and general operating state.
2. P.O.
     Purchase order.
3. MSRP
     Manufacturer's Suggested Retail Price.
4. sales tower
     Term used to describe where the sales managers sit when penciling deals.
5. silver hair

     Car buyers who are senior citizens.
6. hat trick
     Slang used to describe selling three cars in one day.
7. skate
     A term used to describe when a customer is stolen from another salesperson.
8. Term used to describe where the sales managers sit when penciling deals.

TEN

Heresy of Peor

On Sunday night, Leah's thoughts swirled like smoke circles as she lay in bed beside her baby girl. The job ad looked similar to the one she'd responded to, except it added the word Female in front of the phrase Automotive Sales Consultants. It listed recent market changes Tommy Prince mentioned when she brought up the idea to renovate the ladies' rooms.

The ad worked like a charm. Housely and Stalwart interviewed so many female candidates they were able to hire three sales consultants and one Finance Manager.

The newest Finance Manager came from a competitor. She looked like a Nordic supermodel with bright blue eyes and a deep tan. The Supermodel's body was the kind every woman envied because she could wear practically anything, or next to nothing, and it would look expensive. Even though she originally responded to the job ad, she told Leah that Tommy did her a huge favor because he knew she'd fallen on hard times. She'd been a Finance Manager until her husband, the General Manager at the other dealership, banged his advertising rep.

The Supermodel said the homewrecker was her obverse: dark-haired, petite, spunky, and a few years older. Now the Cheerleader, as the Supermodel called the other woman, sported an engagement ring while she nursed her wounds after a nasty divorce settlement. The Supermodel's plan was to move out of Hell Paso as soon as her Austin banker friend came through with a few employment prospects.

Actually, she'd want to go on a Caribbean cruise first and remain inebriated for ten contiguous days. The Supermodel confessed all that upstairs in the ladies' room, moments after she offered Leah a bump of cocaine.

Of the three sales consultants the Managers recruited, one came over from the gentleman's club around the corner. Brittany told Leah she needed to prove one year of sales experience to interview for a pharmaceutical sales job. Her sister had the inside track. When she saw the ad, she remembered Moose and a few of the other men because of their monthly celebration at the club in the wee morning hours. She came in for the interview and, when they invited her to join the sales team, she was so excited she accepted the offer on the spot.

Brittany told Leah a secret and made her swear she wouldn't tell anyone. Of course, Leah promised. She told her Moose said, even if she ultimately decided the car business wasn't for her, she was welcomed to use him as a business reference. As long as she finished one full month of employment at Prince Auto Plaza, he'd confirm one year of sales experience.

As if that weren't enough food for thought, Brittany wanted to share more. As a favor to Moose's fat friend Gerald, she made a special delivery of signed contracts to someone at the Credit Union he wanted her to call Sugar Daddy. When she arrived and asked for Sugar Daddy, the indirect lending clerk understood immediately; it was Gerald's well-known nickname for that particular loan officer.

The clerk called his extension and, in a couple minutes, a straight-laced man came out to greet his visitor. Brittany pressed play on the boom box, gyrated in rhythm to a glam metal band's sex-themed song, and did a striptease down to tassels and a G-string. She left the Credit Union with a surplus of one-dollar bills so, in her opinion, it was a win-win-win for everyone.

Leah's mind returned to the morning when, to her complete horror, she saw Brittany and friends in bikinis on the front curb. Poster boards read, Free Car Wash Until Noon. The double O's in Noon had nipples. They were able to bring in over twenty cars and several prospects for the sales consultants. Later, Leah overheard Finance Managers Henry and Aldo say how impressed they were by Brittany's show of initiative, and they lauded her commitment to the car business.

Another female sales consultant was more subtle about her ambition. Veronica was a driven young woman who had been an El Paso High star basketball player. She kept everything close to the vest except her visible crush on Erik. Leah was concerned something dangerous might brew between those two jocks.

Finally, there was Silke, who was in her late forties. She had a flat tummy, a husky smoker's voice, and spoke with a German accent. Her daily caloric intake consisted of a bag of gummy worms and lots of black coffee. She was recently divorced from the military man she met as a teenager before she became a U.S. citizen. She bragged to everyone in a sales meeting about the complete control she had over a young Army Specialist who lived in her house. He labored for twelve straight hours every Saturday to complete her honey-do list. She declared it had something to do with his lust for a juicy reward.

Leah shut her eyes and let out her anxieties in long, deep, audible sighs. Her overloaded brain gave way to fitful sleep. The rest of her evening was dominated by a troubling vision about a fashion show. In the audience, men in black suits with briefcases in their laps held out one-dollar bills. Their nostrils were covered by a fine, white powder. A never-ending conveyor belt presented stiff models without eyebrows. They dressed in bikini bottoms made of gummy worms and covered their breasts with pom-poms or basketballs.

Instead of a turn at the end of the runway, they hurtled into the screeching abyss.

ELEVEN

Mexican Tailgate Party

L eah forgot to set her alarm. There wasn't time for the entire morning routine. She splashed cold water on her puffy eyes. Brushed her teeth. Put on a clean pair of panties. Threw on the rest of her clothes without the aid of a mirror. Pulled the hair out of her face and into a messy top bun. Ran to the front door without her purse. The top bun bobbed up and down as she hurried back to the bedroom to find it. Noticed her flats didn't match, and selected low heels instead. Paused to take in and push out a couple of deep breaths.

With gratitude, she walked like a sane family member into the kitchen. Kissed her Beka, and Susie, on the cheek. Patted Ralph and the girls on the head. Stole half an everything bagel and dashed out the door to her car.

Three nights prior, a severe thunderstorm came through and wind gusts reached 45 mph. It knocked off the dealership's tallest sign that bore manufacturer logos and dimensional letters that spelled Prince Auto Plaza. Two painted metal poles remained stuck in the asphalt.

The wind left some framework and frayed wires, but not a single sign fragment was found.

Leah slowed the car as she approached. The only other damage she knew of was on the concrete pillar where smokers liked to congregate. It had a deep, diagonal gash at the approximate height of an average adult. The reigning theory was the storm wind threw a plastic shard like a ninja star. There were no injuries since no one was at the up point[1] after hours.

In the last sales meeting, Housely said the dealership would work with the sign company to get a replacement within a few weeks. He also announced he'd divide the sales team into three smaller teams, each with a different start and stop time, effective immediately. Shift changes were meant to address the repeated issue of lack of coverage on the sales floor.

He explained what sounded like an equitable system. Everyone would have the option to leave early, or arrive at work later, several days each month. They could also take a full day off, dependent upon individual performance from the previous month. In return, every team agreed to limit their meal break to thirty minutes max, which would give them time to pick up food for themselves or others. They could eat their meals at their desks, but only when they didn't have customers. Attendance at early morning sales meetings was still mandatory.

As a matter of housekeeping, Housely asked team members to sign a waiver of their right to sue the dealership for any cause. In the event a dispute couldn't be resolved over a cup of coffee, they'd take it to a mediator. He said it would save everyone a bundle on court costs and attorney's fees. Every person obediently signed on the dotted line, though some hesitated at first and debated unspoken consequences.

At the end of the hour, Stalwart asked their special guest to enter. Leah was slack jawed when she saw Old Preacher Johnson come in and lead the room in a slightly modified benediction:

"O Fortune, smile on Montana motor mile. This is what we pray: bless us abundantly every day. Amen."

LEAH WALKED into the air-conditioned showroom and immediately sensed the dread. Managers had vacated the sales tower[2]. She didn't see them anywhere, and she knew it wasn't time for a Save-A-Deal meeting. Brittany assisted a customer at her desk. Other sales consultants loitered about in their spit shine shoes. She heard Gerald's amplified voice at the back of the finance hallway.

"Where is that son of a b——?"

"I wouldn't go back there if I were you," the receptionist warned. Valerie looked dismayed and hid within the confines of the reception station.

Leah walked over to her and retrieved pink message slips from the slot labeled Owers.

"What happened?"

"Aldo didn't put a cash down payment in the overnight safe. Silke saw him buying rounds of drinks at a bar last night."

"Where is he?"

"It's his day off."

Chelsea the finance secretary came out of the hallway. She looked flustered as she rustled through a deal jacket[3]. Jan the Office Manager and her youngest clerk soon followed. They quickly went downstairs together.

Leah moved around the reception station so she could get a better view of the finance hallway. Betty and Stalwart came out of Gerald's office. The woman walked up the stairs that were on that side without a word to her ex-husband. Stalwart's face was almost purple.

Leah had seen that look before.

Housely and Erik came in the side door near service, joined Stalwart, and all three went into the sales tower. Henry and the Supermodel stepped out of their separate glass finance offices and looked lost. A stapler flew through Gerald's doorway and missed the Supermodel's elbow by a centimeter.

Leah's eyes widened.

She looked back at Valerie and waited for her to finish a call transfer.

"Can you tell me about this one?" She handed over a message slip. It was written at 7 a.m., from Mr. Jesus of Wash Guys. The box in front of Wants to See You was checked. Message: Come to BBQ Tailgate in Back Lot at Sunset Today.

"Jesús asked me to invite you. Some of the employees have a get-together a few times a year."

"What should I bring?"

"Nothing, sweetie. You just relax. There will be plenty of food for all of us."

Leah felt lighthearted for a brief moment until Gerald waddled to the end of the hallway. He redirected his ire at them.

"Get him on the phone. Now!"

Valerie obeyed.

AT NOON, Leah saw a disheveled Aldo walk into the showroom. His designer shirt was unbuttoned to the navel and he wore oversized sunglasses that diverted attention away from his sloped forehead. He carried a small metallic case and went downstairs to the ladies' office.

A few minutes passed.

When he reappeared, he still wore his dark sunglasses. She didn't see him speak to anyone. He didn't even stop at the sales tower before he swaggered out of the building to the customer parking lot.

In a few minutes, she and other sales consultants gathered by the window as Aldo's sports car smoldered and did a fishtail. Everyone heard it peel out.

She had respect for the *cojones*[4] on that guy.

HENRY THE FINANCE Manager paged Leah to come to his office. When she arrived, she saw he'd already printed contracts for her customers.

"Ready for them?"

"Not yet. Close the door. I need to talk to you for a moment."

She did as she was told but when she turned around, he stood so close she had to back away to put some distance between them.

"You drive me up the wall."

"What?"

"That top is see-through in the sunlight. You're wearing a red brassiere, aren't you?"

She crossed her arms over her chest.

He snickered and looked through the glass that surrounded his office. There wasn't much privacy.

"Let's go upstairs."

"Absolutely not. I'm going to bring them in now."

His hands reached for her but she sidestepped the issue and gave him the slip.

After Leah's clients signed, they agreed to return the following day so their car could get a full detail. She escaped to the gas station to fill up the gas tank and felt sluggish because she hadn't eaten anything since the half bagel. She bought a hot dog, bag of chips, mint chewing gum, and a cup filled with coffee and ice. The car didn't have to be ready for another twenty-four hours. There was plenty of time.

She parked under a shade tree with the AC on, listened to country music, and took a luxurious thirty-minute work lunch. She awakened refreshed two hours later and used a napkin to wipe the mustard slobber off her chin.

Quite the sexpot.

IT WAS ALMOST sunset and fifteen minutes before the end of her team's official shift. Leah remembered what Housely explained in the last meeting: it would be the sales consultant's choice to either stay late or call it a day. If they were off target for the month, they should stay late. She was on target for her sales goal, but other salesmen on her team indicated they'd work bell-to-bell anyway. If she took off now, she might be perceived by management as an underachiever by comparison.

She went to the back lot, smelled a fiery charcoal grill, and her stomach growled for real food. The guilty feelings diminished. When she moved her car forward close to the service driveway, which was closed for the evening, Susie's station wagon already waited as planned.

Leah scooped precious Beka into her arms while Susie transferred the car seat and put the diaper bag in the trunk. The cousins hugged goodnight. When Susie left, Leah locked her door and pulled on the handle for good measure. She walked around her car with Beka over her hip to check the other three and returned to the driver side to pull once more just in case. Her compulsion was a conscious decision; it felt good to be certain. After she was done, she headed back inside the main building to check out for the night.

She saw two sales consultants talk to the receptionist and her trainee. Donald the Gambler cozied up to the Redhead as Bulldog Ben flirted with the other. Leah could hear their banter as she approached.

"Let me buy you dinner after this."

"No, I can't. I have to go to my second job after I leave here tonight."

"Oh? Where do you work?"

"I'm a cocktail waitress downtown."

"Which bar? I can meet you there. I'll take you out after you get off work."

"No, I'm sorry. I only date women." The Latina brightened when she saw Leah with the little one. "Oh, my gosh. Who's that?"

"This is my daughter, Beka."

Her baby got the Redhead's attention, too.

In an instant, cooing females formed a tight circle and the men were outcasts. Leah thought of Erik, who expected the birth of his son very soon, and looked over at the sales tower. He wasn't there.

***

THE WESTERN SKY was scarlet when she stepped into the make-ready area. *Norteño*[5] music played softly. Strings of white lights illuminated the parking garage. A buffet covered two open truck tailgates. Several employees filled their paper plates. Others drank beer or soda. Jesús waved from the grill. A man in a Texas Longhorns ball cap was next to him but white smoke hid his identity.

Valerie accosted her and zeroed in on the baby.

"What's your name?"

"This is Beka."

"May I hold her, please?"

Her wiggly fingers were already outstretched.

Beka giggled at her new friend.

"Of course!"

They walked around and socialized. Most of the employees were from the service department or the body shop. She didn't see anyone from sales or finance.

Soon Valerie sat in a chair and placed Beka in her lap.

"I'll go fill up our plates," Leah offered. "What would you like to drink?"

"Water or a Mexican Coke, if they have it."

Leah joined the short buffet line and selected a variety of *tacos*[6], *enchiladas*[7], extra *tortillas*[8], with generous toppings of *salsa verde*[9], *pico de gallo*[10], and *crème fraîche*[11]. She wanted to see the selection of grilled meats.

The grill master held up tongs in salutation.

"*Hola*[12], Leah."

"*Hola*, Jesús. *Cómo estás*[13]?"

"*Muy bien*[14]."

Jesús spoke rapid-fire Spanish to his friend in the ball cap.

Ball Cap obeyed and got her another paper plate. He wore a clean white T-shirt and faded jeans. She thought he looked vaguely familiar. He filled her plate with two pre-smoked turkey legs and six slices of seasoned flank steak.

Jesús's grill abilities were impressive. Everything had the perfect amount of char.

When Ball Cap raised his head and made eye contact,

Leah felt a spark of recognition shoot through her veins. He was Jake, Tommy Prince's handyman.

"*Muchas gracias*[15]," she stuttered.

Jesús laughed and peppered more instructions she didn't quite catch.

"I'll help you carry this. What do you want to drink?"

"Two Cokes and two waters."

She waited as Jake managed to get four drinks from the cooler and extra paper towels with his right hand, while he balanced the plate loaded with meats on his left forearm. Jesús monitored his progress and looked at Leah with arched eyebrows.

"By the way, I'm Jake Tanner. And you are?"

"I know who you are. I'm Leah Owers."

"The renovation."

"Yeah."

"We should talk."

"You think?"

"Don't blame me," he surrendered. "I don't own Prince Auto Plaza."

THEY SAT and talked for two hours. Jake played with Beka while Leah and Valerie chowed down. The food was delicious. She discovered the *pico de gallo* was Valerie's home-made recipe. Jake said his butcher shop friend supplied all the meats.

Jesús came by a couple times to see how everything tasted. He took the baby girl in his arms, and they waltzed to the music in 3/4 time as she gazed into the kind man's face.

Leah saw that Jake and Jesús knew each other very well. She was intrigued, and wanted to know their story, so she asked Jake to tell it. After he filled up a plate for himself, he sat down and started in.

He told her he left UT Law after a personal tragedy. That's when he first began to seek out construction jobs, to make ends meet. A friend referred him to the Prince family, and they hired him to do some contract work in Texas and New Mexico. One day, he came to the dealership because Tommy wanted to meet there. He saw Jesús interact with one of his younger wash guys, and recognized him at once.

"Grey around the ears, but the same build and posture, the same voice, I remembered from my childhood. It was a miracle. He came back into my life at the precise moment I needed him most."

His eyes were moist, and Leah saw some hazel mixed in with the green.

"Did he know your father?"

He shook his head.

Back in the 70's, Jesús wasn't a U.S. citizen. He and his associate used to make an illegal border crossing at the early part of spring to travel to a south Texas ranch owned by Jake's distant cousin. Sometimes they'd have to make two or three attempts to get there, but the rancher was patient because they were reliable workers who arrived around the same week every year. He paid the ranch hands generously, by Mexico economic standards, since the *peso*[16] was weaker than the dollar. When winter arrived, Jesús returned to his parents' house with enough money to keep them and his younger siblings comfortable for twelve more months.

Jake's grandparents raised him. They frequently sent the boy to spend summer vacation on the ranch. He loved to ride horses and he'd wander around unsupervised for hours. However, his relatives made the rules clear: anyone who wanted to eat must complete their share of the daily chores. He learned value of a day's work.

Jesús was the ranch hand who showed him how to mend fences around the property. He also taught Jake the signs a ewe was ready to deliver her lambs. In 1980, there was a terrible fire on the ranch. His relatives had to sell and the annual ranch jobs were no more.

Over time, Jesús's siblings got their own jobs and took over financial care of their parents. He fell for one of the lovely Valenzuela sisters, but their courtship was forbidden because he was from the wrong social status. It didn't help matters that he wasn't Roman Catholic either. With the hope hearts and minds would change in due time, they married anyway in a private ceremony conducted by a Spirit-filled missionary.

Unfortunately, the young lady soon became pregnant.

Knowing full well her brothers would rather murder the child than allow a heathen laborer to taint the bloodline, she determined their only chance to be together was to start a new life. Through contacts, she obtained illegal employment as a housemaid at an El Paso physician's house. The doctor arranged for the baby to be born in a U.S. hospital, and his wife sponsored the new family.

The generous American couple also helped them buy a house after they passed the naturalization process. The doctor and his wife were people of faith, from a rich Mexican-American heritage; they became like adoptive parents to the young couple. Their influence solidified Jesús and Gabriella's belief in Providence and their love for the U.S.A.

"Jesús cries when he hears the national anthem," Jake said.

Valerie apologized and said she needed to go. Leah took that as her cue. They said goodnight to Jesús and a few stragglers as Jake started to load everything into a truck.

Baby Beka was sleepy. Leah changed her diaper in the back seat of the Tempo. She didn't need to turn on the cabin light because there was a glare from the showroom windows. Sales remained open for business. She gently lifted Beka into the car seat and double-checked all the fasteners to make sure she'd secured everything. Then she checked all the door locks before she drove away.

Instead of the radio, the hum of tires over pavement became their soundtrack. Beka soon fell sound asleep. In that peaceful moment, Leah reflected upon the story of an unlikely brotherhood between two men, a generation apart. From separate countries. Distinct tribes, and different languages.

Then she realized they never got around to the renovation discussion.

---

1. up point

    A place where a salesperson stands to wait for the next customer who walks on the lot.

2. sales tower

    Term used to describe where the sales managers sit when penciling deals.

3. deal jacket

    A folder that contains all the information in a customer's transaction.

4. *cojones*

    Courage. Literally, "a man's testicles." (Spanish)

5. *Norteño*

    A style of folk music associated with northern Mexico and Texas, typically featuring an accordion and using polkas and other rhythms found in the music of central European immigrants. (Spanish)

6. *tacos*

    A traditional Mexican dish consisting of a small, folded corn or wheat tortilla topped with filling. (Spanish)

7. *enchiladas*

A rolled tortilla with a filling, typically meat, served with a chili sauce. (Spanish)

8. *tortillas*

Round, thin, flat breads of Mexico made from unleavened corn meal. (Spanish)

9. *salsa verde*

A tart sauce made from tomatillos, chili, and cilantro. Literally, "green sauce." (Spanish)

10. *pico de gallo*

Fresh salsa made from finely chopped ripe red tomatoes, white onion, jalapeños, cilantro, lime, and salt. (Spanish)

11. *crème fraîche*

A dairy product similar to sour cream or Mexican crema. (French)

12. *Hola*

Hello. (Spanish)

13. *Cómo estás*

How are you? (Spanish)

14. *Muy bien*

Very good, or very well. (Spanish)

15. *Muchas gracias*

Thank you very much. (Spanish)

16. *peso*

A basic monetary unit of Mexico. (Spanish)

TWELVE

Tampons and Dark Chocolate

Leah was mistaken about something: Menstrual cycles didn't synchronize the way she'd believed for many years. Or, perhaps, women's cycles couldn't sync up in a high testosterone atmosphere. Whatever the reason, there was a deluge of biblical proportions every week of the month. Some called it The Curse or The Red Sea Plague. Others hinted with I'm Riding a Magic Red Carpet, My Kitten has a Bloody Nose, or I Got Shot Again. Her favorite phrase was My Tranny[1] Fluid is Leaking, because it sounded like typical shoptalk.

Hey, guys. The lady said her automobile has a defect. A mechanic can fix that, no problem. Nothing to see here. Move along.

Her desk became a woman's crisis center in a raging war zone: urgent wound care management, pain medication, an occasional hot water-bottle, and plenty of sympathy. Sometimes they came just to talk, which wasn't a surprise. Her gender widely considered her a trusted confidante even as far back as grade school.

Whenever a girl in the schoolyard whispered a secret in her ear, she'd never repeat it. Young Leah's inner principles ultimately worked their way into broad daylight when she was ten. It was her fifth grade year. Mom decided to marry a much older man, and they were to move in with him, so she was uprooted to a different school district in the middle of the year. A mean-spirited girl started bullying her and some of the smaller girls in gym class. Quickly fed up with that nonsense, Leah dropped their victimizer in her tracks.

The school's vice-principal sided with the bully who came from an affluent family. He seemed convinced Leah was the bad seed. Mom reluctantly went along and agreed to a harsh punishment: detention every afternoon in his office until the semester ended. That error put a schism in their relationship. Even if no parent could have guessed at his intention to steal a child's purity, her mother shouldn't have been so careless.

To Leah's credit, she voiced loud dissent about daily detention alone with the vice-principal in his cramped office. Unfortunately, she didn't formulate the right words for what she foresaw and her doe-in-the-headlights mother bought into his psychobabble about tantrums and crocodile tears. She warned Leah to comply with his rules, or else. No daughter of hers would be expelled from the finest academy in the city. It would put her education, and her future, at risk.

She obviously didn't know what the man was capable of.

When cancer overtook her mother shortly thereafter, a hardened Leah went to live with her cousin and enrolled in a public school. Susie and two church youth group leaders eventually helped her find the grace to forgive. Along the way, Leah learned that few adults were equipped with extra sense, and none could be faulted for their lack. She didn't always have it either. The Gift came and went as if it were on a predetermined calendar.

As for Leah's inclination to watch over her peers, it continued after grade school. In high school, she became a lifeguard at the neighborhood waterslide where her friends and their siblings swam. She was pursued by a few suitors but pushed them away. In recent years, she developed a fondness for scuba diving which led her to seek certification as an emergency search and rescue diver.

That's how she'd met Sammy, her first real boyfriend. But their love-at-first-sight moved too fast and was short-lived. She'd thought he returned to the states but, when relatives said they hadn't seen him in months, his dive buddies began the panicky search and found him in the lagoon.

Lately, with the steady stream of young women who confided in her, there were several times she'd been vehemently opposed to their bad choices. If she was too uptight, it was due to a combination of painful life lessons and her newly acquired maternal instinct. However, instead of judgment, she gently voiced caution or disagreement. Then she let it go. People were free to make mistakes. She'd learned plenty by trial and error. The worst thing she could do was tell someone else how to live or love.

The best thing she could do, as a bystander to their misery, was to simply be there for them and tell the truth. After Mom died, she learned about the Maker-Creator and how He patiently called out to sinners' hearts. He was always near, and He didn't mince words. She continued to listen for Father God's voice even though she hadn't heard it in a long while.

That's why she dove into Holy Script.

FOR LEAH, it was easy to gain credibility in another's eyes. Perhaps that's why she did so well in car sales, despite the adversarial nature of the job. With the increased adoption of the Internet, more customers every day were wise to the game. They didn't, for even a second, fall for the ruse that car salesmen were advocates. The jig was up. Yet, customers trusted her. She wasn't manipulative, and she was far from predatory. She truly seemed to care. Those customers who believed she had their best interest at heart weren't disappointed. As she told them repeatedly: her goal was to offer information about their options so they could make a rational decision without any regrets.

In much the same vein, Leah didn't have the skillset to be a two-face. She was the same persona in front of her customer, co-worker, and Manager as she was behind their backs. To her, there was no other way to be; anything else was false. She wouldn't tolerate the rumor mill, either. Not only was gossip a subtle way to denigrate another person–it was a surefire way to maim a life.

Furthermore, she didn't judge by race, creed, gender, politics, or any other differentiator. Everyone received the same level of compassion from her, because each living soul held intrinsic value.

The only thing that might disable her empath-o-meter was if she witnessed an abuse of power. She'd met a few narcissists and sociopaths in her day, but an unusually dense population of both presided over Prince Auto. She was constantly on guard.

<hr>

ALTHOUGH SHE DIDN'T TRUST many of the sales employees, she did her best to get along and she didn't hold grudges. If only they'd come around to her point of view about teamwork, everyone would enrich themselves as well as their neighbor. Work together rather than apart. Quit the oscillation between ally and predator. Don't demand to be made whole after every little task.

Unfortunately for the uninitiated, which wasn't Leah's status anymore, dog-eat-dog was car business tradition. Every man for himself was in their DNA, and they passed it to each generation. Mr. Jameson told her the appropriate response to being skated[2] was to return the favor. Treat others the way they'd treated her. If she wanted it to stop altogether, then she'd have to surprise Yermo in the dark back lot with a baseball bat. Although she could follow rules and procedures with ease, she obviously lacked the savage nature requisite to neutralize barbarians.

Leah was emotionally drained on slow days and she didn't understand the reasons why until she talked it through with Susie. As it turned out, when she wasn't busy, she had more exposure to the verbiage commonly heard in sales huddles throughout the day. When a salesman said, "I ripped his face off," he'd made an insane profit. The aim, let alone the assertion, felt wrong at her very core. When he used phrases like "he dropped his pants," "I bent her over," or "I raped them," he'd gotten the upper hand. Sure, they were merely syllables to express triumph, but they chipped away at her sensibilities. The sum effect of the comments, along with ongoing visions of blood and splatter, was a violent psychological barrage—and she was the shell-shocked soldier.

After further consideration, she outright rejected the bogus notion that something perennial could ever grow out of their foul ideology. The car business could be most accurately depicted by a snake that swallowed its own tail. As an outsider to a culture that had lost all objectivity, she could foresee the futility of its efforts. Therefore, a more personal conundrum accosted her daily: How would any woman be able to secure blessings for her posterity if she fell apart? Or, what would she stand to gain when she cannibalized herself?

SHE'D SEEN the fundamentals of Housely's belief system. If it made gross profit, do it. If it made more gross profit, do that instead. Ethics didn't factor into his computation. She needed to guard her heart from the rot, or it would seep into her soul.

During their argument about the split[3] deal, he didn't condemn Yermo's actions or ask him to apologize to her. Instead, Housely told her to move aside and watch the master. From his vantage point in the sales tower[4], whoever brought him the slaughter was the asset. Whatever lined his pockets with silver and gold mattered the most. She was certain, when he cast his eyes on a person, he saw dollar signs. He gauged everything by that mark; money was an idol.

Leah felt the anger rise again. However, The Holy compelled her to reflect His image. He alone could breathe life into the General Manager, or anyone else for that matter—but it was ultimately a person's choice to accept or reject Him. Love did not force; He was invited. She must draw on His strength and compose herself. Not only was self-control evidence of His indwelling but, in all practicality, it was useful for self-preservation. Housely's level of anger might escalate further if she clashed with his system again. She wasn't naïve; sales consultants came and went all the time. If she wanted to thrive in that career, and reach her financial destination, she must not make waves.

The bohemian flower child must not step in the path

of an oncoming tank to offer a daisy to the enemy. Stay off the radar. Avoid risk.

She had to be shrewd, like an infidel thief who tiptoed through the Cave of Wonders in a cartoon movie. Scratch that, because the thief triggered the cave's collapse and he lost his life. She must utilize her street smarts like the orphaned street rat did. He saw nobody special when he looked at his reflection but he was The Diamond In The Rough. He turned the tables on the greedy villain, saved the kingdom, and won the princess.

Hannah and Sofia loved that movie.

Leah made a mental note to stop by Blockbuster Video and rent it again.

SHE ENTERTAINED herself with her peculiar ideals as she sat behind her desk with nothing to do. After a while, she went for another walk to see what was in the bullpen. She hoped to find a cheap cash car for a young newlywed couple. They couldn't afford to pay more than twenty-two hundred. If she couldn't find anything for them that week, she might sell her Tempo directly to them and finance a new car for herself. Another possibility was to trade in her car and sell it through Prince Auto so it would count as another sold unit.

She decided to put out feelers.

In the back lot, she heard a clang of metal. It was similar to the sound of a lifted and lowered dumpster. Thirty seconds passed and then the sounds of applied brakes were followed by a creaky crunch and tinkle of shattered glass. She didn't hear a heavy duty garbage truck engine, or backup beepers, so she wondered what it might be.

When she rounded a corner by the collision center, she saw a scene unfold through the chain link fence that halted her in her tracks. The rear of a large black SUV was jammed up against the back of another black SUV. Both appeared to be the current model year. Stalwart got out of one and climbed into the driver's seat of a white SUV. Then he drove forward a short distance while Roberto and Housely stood aside without a concern.

Stalwart shifted, reversed, and struck another white SUV behind him. Her heart leaped into her throat and her jaw slackened its grip.

Two service porters loitered by the same fence, at the rear of the adjacent service department building. They'd observed the same thing and seemed to have absorbed the shock. She made eye contact with them and walked over.

"What's this? The demolition derby?"

The smoker shook his head at her.

"Naw."

"Then what's going on in there?"

"Moose is just keeping Tommy Prince in a positive cash flow situation."

She saw no reason for sarcasm.

He stabbed out the cigarette butt on a short rock wall and put it in his pocket. The paging system clicked a few times so he nodded an unspoken message at his cohort and jogged into the building.

The other porter was the young man who'd introduced her to the Farmer. He saw the confusion in her eyes and took pity on her.

"It's more revenue for the body shop and parts."

"That doesn't make sense."

"The insurance company will pay for it."

"But won't premiums go through the roof?"

"Not if the windstorm caused the damage."

1. tranny
    Colloquial name for "transmission."
2. skate
    A term used to describe when a customer is stolen from another salesperson.
3. split
    A term used to describe when the commission on a car deal is divided up between two salespeople.
4. sales tower
    Term used to describe where the sales managers sit when penciling deals.

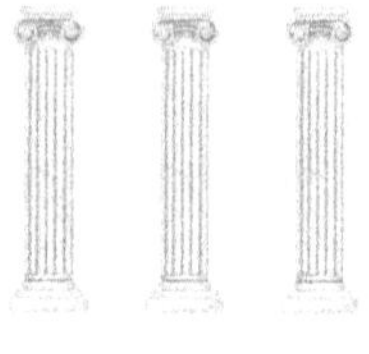

THIRTEEN

Jackassery

Leah didn't find any cash cars in the bullpen so she'd have to try again another day. For the time being, she'd distance herself from unlawful activities in the back lot. She planned to nose around later and visit Flor at the body shop. They'd met briefly at the tailgate party.

She went by the busy make-ready area and headed over to Luxury Imports. Someone picked up the dealership-wide paging system.

"Amanda Lay. Looking for Amanda Lay. Come to the reception desk," a female announced. It sounded like the young initiate's voice.

Amanda Lay? Must be a crank call.

Less than a minute passed, and the paging system picked up again.

"Seymour Butz. You have a call on line number two."

Leah heard laughter from far away. She couldn't believe those jokers at the Truck Center. It was the middle of a workday, with customers everywhere.

"Mike Hunt," the new page started but ended abruptly. There was a click and no further sound.

"Numbskulls."

———

SHE WALKED into the tiny Luxury Imports showroom and smelled the eucalyptus sachets Shelley liked to tuck out of sight. Classical music played overhead. Usually at least one person was stationed within eyesight of the front and side doors but no one was around. Shelley had two full-time employees: Nick, a UTEP Miners football star turned sales pro, and Timothy who was their special needs lot attendant.

A glance into Shelley's small office, and then she returned to the showroom to look out all the floor-to-ceiling windows. No sign of life outside, except a few crimson-stained cigarette butts in the sand ashtray. The last place to check was the unisex bathroom.

Three knocks on the door, but there was no answer. She opened it and entered to do a quick checkup of her appearance in the small bathroom mirror.

On a previous visit, Leah asked Shelley about Timothy's story. He was twenty-three and still lived with his adopted parents. He had shown signs of high intelligence at three years old. Psychiatrists didn't understand Autism back then. One day, he read an article about foreign cars and became infatuated with a particular OEM[1] in Europe. Precisely the same vehicles they sold at the Luxury Imports showroom. He caught the Sun Metro every other weekday to visit the cars. Timothy consumed every brochure, or any other reading materials Shelley could provide. He memorized every factoid and could recall every dimension or specification upon request.

After two birthdays passed, Shelley offered him a job. She needed someone who could gently detail new vehicles and make them ready for display. It was a low volume store so he wouldn't have too many pressures. His parents were almost as thrilled as he was.

The only accommodation he asked for was to be able to wear his earphones. He liked to keep them on because they made him feel secure. Shelley agreed to the terms, and he began his new job immediately.

Leah thought it was possible that Timothy was scheduled to be off. If so, she was sorely disappointed because he liked to chat incessantly about cars. He'd tell her obscure facts accessible only to people who worked at the factory or in a parts department. The names of discontinued exterior colors for a particular model and year. How many coats of paint the manufacturer sprayed on every car. Where the interior materials originated. The specific stitch sewn into the seat coverings. His memory was like a bear trap and it astonished her. Some of the Managers called him Rain Man, a character in a movie about a savant.

"Hello?"

One more look.

She walked back to the windows. It was highly irregular. She'd have to leave a post-it note on Shelley's desk and come back another time. She turned toward the office and paused at the doorway when she saw Chanel Vamp nails grasp the edge of the walnut executive desk. Then the top of a dirty blonde wig rose behind the hand.

"Shelley!"

The Luxury Manager's head snapped up and she muttered something. It took her a minute to get into her leather chair. With her wig askance and mascara smudged, she'd seen much better days.

"Sorry, my carpet has a rip. Just had it installed, too. Going to raise Hell."

Leah thought Shelley looked a little distracted. She didn't seem like herself. What made matters worse: the air in that room was oppressive.

Should get a rotating fan in here.

"What can I do for you, love?"

"I wanted to see if Nick has any interesting trades coming in."

It wasn't a lie. She was really here to visit Timothy but she'd also want the scoop about potential quality pre-owned units if Nick were there. She sensed it was not a very good time for Shelley. Anyway, she probably should try to catch another prospect before her next appointment arrived. It would be her turn at the up point[2] soon. She should leave.

"What do your customers—?"

"Forgive me. I forgot something. Got to run."

She backed away.

"Call you later!"

When she got outside, she inhaled a deep breath of relief and speed-walked to the main showroom. The last split second of Shelley's expression had given her the impression she'd wanted her to go away.

What did I do to annoy her?

Maybe the woman could use some dark chocolate in her life. Leah exhaled, then slowed her stride as she remembered Shelley didn't have monthly cycles anymore. She'd had a hysterectomy while she was in the Air Force.

Somewhere, back in the direction of the Lux Showroom, a man cursed. Leah spun around and nearly stumbled at the sight. There was Nick, the linebacker, on the patio. With Shelley.

From what large hidey-hole did he crawl out of?

Shelley smoothed down her unruly bangs and lit a cigarette. Nick guzzled a bottle of water and slapped his Manager's rear-end.

Oh, my.

Leah turned back toward the main showroom. She didn't want to make a hasty assumption; Shelley was Stalwart's longtime girlfriend. An impure thought buzzed her conscience but she swatted it away. It returned and persisted. Nick. Behind Shelley's desk?

No.

Leah approached the smooth colonnade as Chuck left the up point pillar to greet a prospect. They high fived as they passed each other, and she claimed the vacant spot. Henry aka Wet Willy and Moose Stalwart stood together near the diagonal slice in the pillar. Henry prated on about a business matter, while Stalwart puffed smoke and stalked his Luxury Manager girlfriend from afar. Flushed cheeks betrayed his solemnity. Henry didn't seem to notice. Fed up, Stalwart stubbed out his nicotine stick in the sand tray and turned toward the door. Undeterred, Henry started to follow but changed course when he saw Leah.

His eyes dragged from her pointy boots up to her bosom.

She was confident in her appearance because she'd just checked herself in the mirror. A nude-colored camisole camouflaged her white bra. There was nothing seductive about her outfit, and she wouldn't be humiliated again.

"I can see the color of your bra."

"No, you can't. Pound sand."

She was tired of his drivel.

CHUCK CAME by Leah's desk when his shift ended. He was done with Prince Auto and on his way out. He and Linda would start a new venture on Monday. Before he was able to state the last part of his news, she jumped up and gave him a big hug. She'd miss him dearly.

She'd guessed he was unhappy at the dealership, but she had no idea about the exit strategy. He explained he'd operate a mortgage brokerage on the outskirts of town that specialized in first-time and subprime buyers.

"Are you ready for your dream house?"

"Ever the consummate sales professional."

"I can get you a decent, low rate."

"Payments no higher than a car payment with no money down? Dream house, here I come!"

"And, don't forget, I have a wholesale furniture guy."

"I'll never buy retail again."

"Walk out with me?"

"Only if you don't flip the bird at Managers. I still need this job."

It was already sunset. Time for the daily ritual. She retrieved her car keys and locked the drawer. She yanked on the handle to check. It didn't open, but she reinserted the key anyway to unlock it, and locked it once more. Another tug. Now she was certain everything was secure.

As Chuck and Leah approached the doors, a gorgeous —and very pregnant—young woman walked to the sales tower[3] and gave Erik a flat box the size of a small pizza. Leah tugged Chuck's sleeve and they stopped to gawk. Erik looked embarrassed about the extra attention he received from the onlookers. He opened his present. It was a chocolate chip cookie-cake with icing that read Happy Birthday Honey.

"I didn't know it was your birthday!" Leah exclaimed.

She introduced herself and her co-worker Chuck to

Mrs. Harrison, whose name was Leesa. The baby was due any hour. That inspired a quip from Chuck about men's unlimited capacity for sports stats, but their inability to remember important dates. Erik seemed to appreciate the dig, and Leesa clutched her belly as she laughed.

Leah liked her and could see why Erik said fidelity with his wife meant more than loyalty to anyone else. She hoped to see her again and become friends.

HALF AN HOUR LATER, Chuck and Leah walked toward the unlit back lot.

"Before I go, I have to tell you about something. You're going to hate me."

"Did I do something?"

"No, you didn't do anything wrong. At least I don't think you did, but what I believe doesn't matter."

"What is it?"

"You need to know the rumor."

"What rumor?"

Chuck inhaled deeply through his nose and exhaled slowly.

"Chen thought he saw you giving pleasure to Carlos in his car."

She was taken aback.

"For the record, Carlos didn't deny it or try to correct him."

Leah thought back to the night of the Mexican restaurant. Carlos, in a rush to leave. The delay when he reclined his seat. Then he asked her to recline her seat as well so they could gaze up at the stars together.

"Also, lots of salesmen lost their bets because they thought you wouldn't do it. Now they think you're easy."

He set me up.

"Mother trucker!"

Her voice echoed through the parking garage.

---

1. OEM

    Original Equipment Manufacturer.

2. up point

    A place where a salesperson stands to wait for the next customer who walks on the lot.

3. sales tower

    Term used to describe where the sales managers sit when penciling deals.

Flor's Story

Flor, the front counter agent at the body shop, liked to describe her position as an exalted administrative assistant. She invited Leah and Beka over for lunch on Sunday afternoon, at her small, coral pink house on El Paso's south side. She'd prepared chicken Jerusalem and garlic flatbread. Leah tossed strawberry spinach salad with raspberry vinaigrette, as Flor poured ice water from a pitcher into two glass tumblers. In the living room, Beka sat in the playpen and sampled an appetizer of soft building blocks.

The table was set, and the women sat down together. They enjoyed each other's company. The chicken was perfectly moist and delicious. Leah asked for seconds. When they'd finished lunch, Flor led in an after-meal blessing.

"Blessed are you, LORD our God and Master of the universe. You give bread to all flesh, for Your mercy endures forever."

She'd never heard anyone pray quite like that before.

"And through Your great goodness we have never

lacked, nor will we lack food forever, for the sake of Your great Name. Blessed are You, LORD, who nourishes all. Amen."

Leah cleared everything as Flor hand-washed dishes in a deep farmhouse sink. When they checked on Beka, they marveled because the angel had already fallen fast asleep. They tiptoed back into the kitchen. Flor asked her to sit for a while so she could share a personal testimony. Leah remarked that other people's stories had recently become a pastime.

Flor looked serenely into her eyes. Fifteen to twenty seconds passed before she began.

"Has anyone ever talked to you about human trafficking?"

Leah shook her head.

"In the United States of America, we have more slaves today than there were before or during Abraham Lincoln's presidency."

"What?"

"Yes, it's true. I volunteer with an organization that rescues women and children from traffickers who supply the high demand for young sex workers. It's a criminal enterprise, more profitable than the multi-billion dollar drug industry."

FLOR REVEALED she was a recovered alcoholic and drug addict. She grew up without a father. Her mother was a wanderer. As a young child, she fended for herself. She used to steal food and other items. Nobody monitored her whereabouts. No one seemed to ever see her. Sometimes she convinced herself she had the power of invisibility and, if she concentrated harder, she could make herself disappear.

When she turned fourteen, she skipped school several times to be with a boyfriend who was twice her age. He said all the right phrases, bought her nice things, and deflowered her. He promised to give her the moon if she'd run away with him. Of course, she went willingly; he was her ticket out of *El Chuco*[1]. Little did she know about the real world back then.

The man drove west on I-10. They arrived in Scottsdale late in the evening. He said they'd crash at an uncle's house overnight, and then continue the drive in the morning. He told her not to be worried if the place was full of his relative's friends; everyone was welcomed, so people came and went all hours of the day or night.

It was a nice neighborhood. The house was average, single story with three bedrooms and two baths. A group watched cable TV. Flor went to the back bedroom and fell asleep. The man remained in the living room. In the middle of the night, she wanted a drink of water. It sounded like people were still in there, and some were in the front yard where a stereo blared heavy metal. She walked through the living room to access the kitchen. The TV transmitted X-rated content. Her boyfriend followed her and forced her to have intercourse against a counter in full view of others.

When he finished, she removed herself from that side of the house. She closed the bedroom door and saw it didn't have a lock. Her jumbled thoughts tried to make sense of what just happened. Perhaps he was drunk, or he had some bad drugs in his system. She was certain her boyfriend loved her and figured he'd sober up by morning.

She was tragically wrong on both fronts.

The next morning, the man told her he needed to pay

off a gambling debt before he could move on. For the next two weeks, he sold her to strangers who paid to use her. If she didn't comply, he struck her repeatedly until she did. She wanted to die. It wasn't until she discovered padlocks on the bedroom windows that she realized he'd never been her boyfriend; he was her kidnapper.

Every couple months after that, the man moved her from city to city along the I-10 corridor. They went as far west as Riverside, California all the way east to Jacksonville, Florida. They lived in countless hotels and motels from coast to coast. To make her more docile, and less of a runaway risk, the man injected illicit drugs into her bloodstream. The drugs helped her escape her body; she didn't feel pain or shame.

She was trafficked to thousands of clients; yet, none cared that she was underage. No one questioned her bruises. The police never kicked in the door to save her. The man burned her with a cigar to mark her *quince años*[2]. She was chattel.

On a rainy Monday morning in September, Flor dreamed the man went into cardiac arrest and expired on a musty couch. She was in a drug-induced stupor at the time. It took several hours before she came to herself and made the 911 call. She wouldn't leave the motel room until a compassionate social worker persuaded her it was safe to go outside.

"That woman released me from mental bondage by telling me I could be part of Heaven's plan to save many prisoners. She took me in, cleaned me up, and helped me study for the high school equivalency exam so I wouldn't return to the darkness. Now I'm a sex trafficking survivor and I've dedicated my life to this cause. For the rest of my days, I will help others find out why they're alive."

HER PERSONAL ACCOUNT meant more than anything else Leah had heard in such a long time. It resurrected the feelings that had inspired her to be a devoted rescue diver. Bottom line: Leah also yearned to save people from murky waters. A profound longing in her chest ached like a fresh heartbreak. Tears streamed down her face.

The two women hugged and prayed beside the kitchen island. They talked for hours like soul sisters. The discussion centered on their similar *raison d'être*[3] or *ikigai*[4], a Japanese concept.

While Flor changed Beka's diaper, she educated Leah about why they'd never be fulfilled by a job or a six-figure income: because they knew Him. Nothing else could compare. Even though they might feel He was far away for a season, they'd met the ever-present, Almighty Knower and He was enough.

The Holy was an unfamiliar Spirit to inhabitants of the mortal plane who believed paper money was more useful than Holy Script. A large percentage of the population held to a worldview that glimpses of eternity were implausible, therefore, they capitalized on the defenseless here and now. Those with the most damnable thoughts were empty houses where a myriad torments resided.

Leah and Flor agreed if they didn't need the paycheck they'd quit their jobs in a heartbeat. What a privilege it would be to pursue their passion or mission full time. In the meanwhile, they had to face the age old tug-o-war. Money vs. Love. Choose Money, and pay the bills. Choose Love, and be destitute. If only there were a third option:

Become wealthy and do whatever you want.

1. *El Chuco*
   Nickname for the city of El Paso. (Spanish)
2. *quince años*
   Fifteenth birthday. (Spanish)
3. *raison d'être*
   The most important reason or purpose for someone's existence. Literally, "reason for being." (French)
4. *ikigai*
   A concept about direction or purpose that makes life worthwhile. Literally, "reason to live." (Japanese)

Car-Man the Magnificent

Leah could still hear the exhortation to stay away from "The Ring of Fire." That was what Flor called the group that consisted of Roberto, Housely, Stalwart, and others. Whether it was past trauma or precognition, her bones felt something wasn't right.

Her suspicions seemed justified based on a few observations. Housely brought the same small suitcase to Roberto at least once a week, and a stranger would pick it up at the end of the workday. Last summer, her Manager had gotten stinky drunk at his backyard barbecue and bragged to employees that the inground pool installation was on Tommy Prince's dime. She also overheard his speaker phone discussion with the Comptroller and the General Manager about their fifty thousand dollar swimming pools.

Since it was Monday, Leah tried hard to refocus on her job duties. She scrambled to prepare for delivery of a Certified Pre-Owned 4-door sedan while the young married couple signed financial paperwork. Thanks to Car-Man the Magnificent, Leah's nickname for the

General Manager, the couple agreed to finance their first car loan. They'd originally intended to buy a cash car with their meager savings until Housely called Leah over to the sales tower[1].

She was annoyed when he made her wait there for a few minutes while he finished something else. Then he asked her why she hadn't closed[2] her customers yet. She explained there were no trouble-free cars on the planet in their price range. Housely looked to Stalwart, who nodded to confirm that was indeed a fact. The General Manager motioned for her to come closer, and instructed her exactly what to say about a particular CPO[3] unit. Their monthly payments wouldn't be any higher than one eighty-nine per month if they put down the tax, title, and license. TT&L would be less than half their savings, so they'd still have money left over for a rainy day.

She repeated that to the newlyweds, and explained the benefits of a CPO. The couple looked at each other with wild anticipation and said they wanted to take a test drive[4]. She got them to agree to terms while they were still on the road.

When Erik returned to work the day after his son was born, the Managers moved him out of the sales tower and under the tutelage of Frank at the Truck Center. Without a junior Manager to delegate tasks to, the General Manager became more involved in every car deal and emerged as Car-Man the Magnificent, the next seer and soothsayer of a new age. His psychic abilities were eerily on point.

Brittany, Silke, and Veronica extolled their mystical encounters with Car-Man the Magnificent. Brittany claimed he told her to ask a female customer if she had a rich uncle who would co-sign for her. That's all it took, and everything fell into place. Silke said when Housely proposed the Credit Union's promotional interest rate, something clicked, and her customers gave in to the deal. Veronica, now going by the nickname Ronnie, was still amazed at what Housely's instructions did for her dead-as-nails car deal. In the middle of a negotiation, he told her to borrow Brittany's push-up bra. While Brittany went braless, he instructed Ronnie to let her hair down and apply red lipstick. She did so, and her customer signed that very evening.

"I guess he's right. Sex sells."

LEAH WAS uneasy when Ronnie asked for a transfer to the Truck Center. Her apprehension was more for Erik than anyone. He had a newborn, but he was required to spend ungodly chunks of time away from his family. It would be a challenge for any marriage, but she was especially worried because he stacked the odds against himself. He was so darn friendly to almost everyone. Some women, herself not included, might interpret his accessibility as a sign of his availability. Few men in his position could resist the advances of a female aggressor who planned her attack, and sealed all the exits prior.

She couldn't relate to the mindset that would set out to gut a marriage, but she knew the car business cloyed with it. The Truck Center was down by one Chihuahua, due to Tito's recent departure to pursue a management opportunity at an insurance agency. Ronnie was likely to have her way soon; the General Manager's decision was imminent.

LEAH WANTED to be part of a solution, not part of the problem, but she didn't know where to begin. The male-female issue was enormous, and it would remain hidden because the public would find it disreputable. For example, those "Sexcapades." Most of the salesmen, and Silke in particular, boasted about sales conquests in the filthiest oration possible. Before long, the competition consistently devolved into an opportunity to showboat their sexual exploits—as if it were crucial to ascertain the biggest fornicator in the realm. It got so rambunctious; no one could speak in normal tones. They had to remove their discourse from the showroom and relocate upstairs.

On the other side of things; some employees were quiet about their shame. The process always involved elements of guilt, humiliation, and self-contempt. When women came to Leah's desk to divulge their secrets, they did it in the same way they'd wrap a used tampon in toilet paper before it was discarded. Like they'd conceal a prohibited item in a brown paper bag. Quiet and discreet. Eventually, it seemed, individual female employees couldn't resist the need to articulate, self-examine, and be debriefed about sin. As if each had a compunction. A small inner voice.

On those occasions, Leah maintained a neutral expression so as not to reward poor choices. Instead, she offered constancy and the desirable curative properties of dark chocolate with high cacao content. She responded with sympathetic eye rolls whenever they steamed about Prince Auto men's micro assaults of condescension. When they inundated her with accounts of when men had debased, mistreated, misused, and exploited them she didn't know what else to do but pray silently.

The women knew their secrets were safe with her and, most important, that she believed them. They had no reason to lie. If she chose to doubt even one, she must discredit them all, and she wasn't willing to consider the entire group as pathological.

However, regardless of how much Leah talked sense to them, each felt partially responsible for the escalation of abuses. In retrospect, every woman fully participated in an initial indiscretion and had since become inured to it. Several attractive climbers went along reluctantly to prove loyalty to the ones in power. Others were young, single moms who sought to ingratiate themselves with men of financial means. Most earnestly hoped to connect with a mentor or a provider. Every one feared reprisal.

She wondered if those men had any notion their misdeeds blasted into the aether in much the same way Mexican stations broadcast a *telenovela*[5] to *abuelita's*[6] TV. At any rate, the Managers were likely to deny wrongdoing. Even if two or three from the riffraff sounded an alarm, the establishment would surely eliminate them. No one dared to speak against the system.

SHE WATCHED as Hannah and Sofia built a tower of wooden blocks. According to the tabletop game instructions, every layer must assimilate to a prescribed pattern. Stack one, two, three blocks left to right. Turn ninety degrees. Repeat. Each level depended on the level beneath to hold up. Remove the wrong game piece and it was touch and go; lose too many and the tower would be unstable. If one level couldn't depend on another, the tower of blocks would crumble. Clear the table and start over. Stack them one, two, three. Left to right.

The repetitive procedure opened an esoteric window for her. Managers routinely tested employees to determine if they were dependable, or necessary to the structure, and could remain in play. Otherwise, they were to be ejected. First, they'd arrange a transaction. Scratch my back and

I'll scratch yours. A favor for a favor. A *quid pro quo*[7]. After a while, a minimum tax of blood, sweat, and tears was expected in exchange for a share of the spoils. Much later, after every drop was bled and every ounce drained or milked, more would be required from the ones who remained in the game. They'd relinquish their dry wooden selves to the pyre and leave nothing behind but ashes.

She was ensconced in her meditative state when she entreated Father of Lights to reverse the desolation of souls. His answer came in an accelerating succession of pictures, like a strobe-like zoetrope of a bygone era. Throughout millennia, ignoble men and women gave their lives for causes like Liberty, Justice, or Love. But, apparently, at Prince Auto, they raised gilded chalices to the Automotive Wall of Shame. Their rallying cry was Eat Today, Die Tomorrow. There were no such things as birthrights in the car business—unless you were a Prince.

JAKE LOOKED at Leah with a sober expression.

"Let's talk. Follow me."

"Thought you'd never ask."

She compelled her mouth not to grin from ear to ear. It was no use; she couldn't help herself. He wasn't around very often. The man was busy with so many different projects at multiple properties.

She followed him to the back of the hallway by the Finance Director's office. Gerald had shut his thick wood door for privacy, as he often did for Save-A-Deal meetings. All the other finance offices had glass windows and she didn't see any Managers. They were holed up in Gerald's office and were likely to be in there for more than an hour.

Jake led the way upstairs. When they reached the top,

they went through the dim corridor and passed by the vacant finance secretary's office, dealer principal's office, conference room, and advertising manager's office. After a few unused rooms, they came to the Comptroller's office at the end. Her vertical blinds were closed. Then they went out a door and into an alcove. It sometimes served as an overflow for service customers but they were alone. The door to the ladies' room was to their right.

He turned to face her. She noticed his pleasant, clean scent.

"Betty gave me feedback on the plans."

As if he'd just taken a shower…

"So we're making the Truck Center unisex."

Very unlike how a sweaty, shirtless handyman would smell…

"Is there anything you'd like to see in this one?"

She blinked.

"A table or a pullout tray to change a diaper."

He nodded.

"And a cabinet to put extra toiletry items."

"Jan told Betty you suggested that. Won't be a problem."

"Great!"

He didn't budge.

She couldn't think. Seconds ticked by.

"There's something I have to tell you."

"What the—?" she yelled. Apparently, Chen could trot halfway around the globe before Carlos could set the record straight.

"Sshhh! Please, I'm in a quandary."

Oh. It wasn't about the rumor.

"If I don't show you, you'll be in danger."

She scrutinized his face.

"But if I do, you could still be in danger. You. Can't. Tell. Anyone."

No renovation could possibly be that serious.

His eyes implored her to respond.

"I know. Snitches get stitches. That's why they busted Nancy Kerrigan's kneecap."

"Hold on. I thought they committed aggravated assault, criminal solicitation, and conspiracy to give Tonya Harding a chance at Olympic gold."

"Hmmm."

"You may have a point."

"Did you know they thought about killing Kerrigan?"

He shook his head.

"But someone didn't want to wreck his car."

"What do you think she snitched about?"

"I think Harding stole someone's wax."

"To land the triple axel, huh?"

"No, not ice skater's wax."

He blinked a couple times.

"Hair removal. A girl with that much testosterone can't afford to skip her waxing regimen."

His eyes twinkled. He finally cracked a smile.

There you are. She tilted her head and admired his handsome face.

He gently touched her elbow and led her back through the corridor.

Her upper arm brushed against his chest but she shoved the sensation from her mind.

Moments later, they quietly circled the bottom of the steps to a utility closet underneath the stairwell. Leah hadn't known it existed. Jake kept a lookout to ensure there were no witnesses. He unlocked the door, opened it, and shined a mini flashlight into the shadows so she could see.

She didn't immediately understand what she saw. There were stacks of electronics, several wires, and LED lights. Some of the equipment appeared to be VCR players. After further inspection, she discerned they were VHS cassette recorders.

He closed the door and locked it again. Without a word, he placed an index finger over his lips and pointed toward the showroom. Then he pointed at his eyes and his ears. He finished with a fingertip over his lips again.

Her eyes enlarged as her wisdom increased. She covered her mouth with her hand.

Jake motioned for her to come closer. With his face next to her ear, she could almost taste the grape jelly sandwich he must have devoured for lunch. Childhood nostalgia calmed her emotions. In the moment, she felt free and uninhibited enough to close her eyes.

"I'll be praying for you," he breathed.

----

1. sales tower
   Term used to describe where the sales managers sit when penciling deals.
2. close
   Term to describe the act of convincing a customer to agree to a sales transaction.
3. CPO (Certified Pre-Owned)
   A used vehicle that has been inspected and refurbished by the dealer.
4. test drive
   Driving of a motor vehicle to determine its drivability or roadworthiness, and general operating state.
5. *telenovela*
   Latin American serial drama similar to a soap opera. (Spanish)
6. *abuelita*
   Familiar name for a grandmother. (Spanish)
7. *quid pro quo*
   An exchange of goods or services. (Latin)

SIXTEEN

Dragon Lady

At midnight, Leah and the Firefighter's buddy climbed into Housely's backyard to scuba dive in the unlit swimming pool. There were stars on the water. She'd forgotten his name, or where they'd first met, but she was sure they'd submerged together before. It wasn't until the middle of the pre-dive checklist, when she tugged weight pouches to ensure they were secure, that she realized none of it was real. Even so, she obeyed safety guidance and finished every step. When she indicated she was ready to begin, they pulled down their masks and slipped under the surface together.

She didn't need a scuba light as her skin glowed in the wetsuit. The vast, empty ocean floor spread out below without any boundary but the inky edge of visibility. The other diver motioned that he wanted to swim in a particular direction, so she followed him. After a few minutes, she saw a dying red sun suspended in the soundless deep. They swam for quite a while through car exhaust and brake dust, until they could observe dramatic details of the stellar arena.

Four incandescent cowboys on horseback corralled a maiden. She wore a red gingham dress and her tresses went down past her waist. Her feet were covered in soot. Gilded lariats constrained the pitiful creature's arms and torso. She seemed afraid one moment, then grievously bipolar the next. Her tense face gave way to ferocity, and quickly changed to a fixed lipstick smile as if she were winner of the 10th Annual Junior Miss Strawberry Pageant. A ruby tiara magically appeared on her head but the weightless creature continued to vacillate.

She shifted into six subsequent natures, and each mercurial beast wore a self-appointed diadem: An opera singer in a red ball gown; an androgynous warrior in a red silk kimono; a red goddess on lotus petals; a red leathered dominatrix with tusks; a siren with red pearlescent scales; a courtesan with a thousand meters of crushed red velvet attached to her fitted bodice.

The afflicted beauty clicked through mediums as if they were TV channels. Her intensity grew, but the posse held on tightly from the four cardinal directions. Meteors from a faraway nebulae rushed to the courtesan's aid. Leah's dive buddy transformed into an indomitable star lord and established a circular shield from the impending attack. He also pushed against an encroachment of dark matter by himself. His peers arrived to join in the skirmish. Illumined brothers in arms were drawn into duels for the sake of honor.

Lest the cosmos implode, white jet fire shot from Heaven's throne room straight through the middle of the bullseye. The might of a thousand suns simultaneously released the apostate and repelled her to a nether plane. She fell in slow-motion fury as co-conspirators grasped at her train of excess and were dragged down to the depths.

LEAH FELT warm water between her legs. Her belly obstructed a direct view but she saw the familiar Saltillo tile at *Isla Navidad*[1]. She was certain her water just broke.

Like judo punches to her lower back, she felt the indisputable first round.

Aaaggh!

Three short breaths, one long: *Whoo, whoo, whoo. Whoo-two-three.*

She had to track the space between contractions. The wall clock's second hand sped rapidly around the dial. *No, no, no.* It was all wrong. She must find a soft bed where she could birth her child properly.

A vague memory of a lush lawn behind a wall of shrubbery made her approach the French patio doors. She passed her circus mirror reflection and thought the bleach white bath robe and sparkling rhinestone barrettes accentuated her pregnancy glow nicely. Then she went outside and found a male doula with a pile of velvety towels. He was ready to assist. Though there was an artifice to his presence, something awfully familiar about those red eyes, she was desperate.

Soon they found a private area on the green grass. She lay down and raised her knees.

Aaaggh!

Whoo, whoo, whoo. Whoo-two-three.

She was fully dilated. It was time, so she took a deep breath and pushed for six or seven seconds. Her helper crouched into a baseball catcher's position and squarely called her every synonym for a loose woman.

Suddenly, a sparrow flew out of her birth canal and up into the sky. It turned into a small yellow plane that distributed a slurry of seeds over aerated lands. Leah was suddenly transported to an eagle eye view. She watched a flightless red hydra bound after her grown daughter, and laughed through her tears as Beka stealthily evaded the predator whose many heads failed to reach consensus.

Beka ran into a desert hiding place that had been prepared by and for faithful guardians. The hydra tried to drown her in rivers that poured out of many mouths, but the thirsty earth absorbed every drop. Frustrated, the serpent went off to demolish others.

Leah awakened to the sound of her clock radio and the sensation of supple baby hands around her thumbs.

---

1. *Isla Navidad*
     Name of a place in Mexico. Literally, "Christmas Island." (Spanish)

SEVENTEEN

Worse Than a Telenovela

Leah stayed away from the dealership for two days. She'd never called in sick before. The discovery of illegal wiretaps was the likely cause of her recurring stomach cramps. Jake hadn't told her the specifics, and she never got to interrogate him. In fact, they hadn't spoken a word to each other since they walked down that finance hallway and parted ways in the showroom.

She'd formulated her own theory anyway, based on cumulative observations: Jake's white Jeep and the contractor van on the day of the install; Jake's pleas with Housely the following day; Housely's headphones and his sudden magical insight; Car-Man the Magnificent, the con man aka Will Housely.

Psychic abilities. Yeah, right.

Principalities didn't long to look into car deals. It wasn't on their agenda.

She'd never questioned management's decision to have cameras in the showroom. Why would she? What was so strange was the lack of security everywhere else. There were no cameras to watch over the extensive number of vehicles in inventory. No cameras in service, parts, or at the body shop. Nothing in the finance hallway, nor by the vault in the ladies' office downstairs. Nowhere else on the property, yet Housely went through a lot of trouble to record both audio and video in the showroom.

Does Erik know? It was impossible that Stalwart would be oblivious to Housely's scheme.

Customers had a general expectation of privacy. She was aware of hundreds of circumstances when a Prince Auto sales employee left customers by themselves, but the dealership hadn't posted a warning that conversations were recorded. Leah knew her legal knowledge was limited, but she'd obtained some nuggets from movies or TV crime shows she'd seen over the years. If Texas had a law against audio recordings without proper disclosure, which she was sure the state did, then each incident was a violation. And, since Jake had studied law, perhaps that's what his argument with Housely in the used car lot was about.

She agonized over the employee-to-employee interactions that took place at her desk when she wasn't with customers. How much did Housely hear live? Did he keep recordings, or did he reuse old tapes? Did someone else listen to the playback? She was as miserable as a driver pulled over for an unknown traffic citation.

If only there were a way she could determine how much Housely knew. As for future confessions, she wouldn't allow any more in the showroom. She resolved to take the women to the restroom or outside for a walk, but she wouldn't tell them why. Jake was right: If she told anyone about the audio recordings it could lead to her termination, or worse. Sexual misconduct was only a symptom of their moral depravity. If they were willing to dip a toe in that far, they could already be nose deep in illegal activities. Eavesdropping, fraud, and embezzlement might be the tip of a criminal iceberg. She could identify a few rapacious actors, but not all. Who knew how bad the worst of them were, or what they might do to her family if she meddled in their business?

Leah's concerns returned to the women who'd confided in her. She'd found common ground in the sisterhood; their vulnerabilities were universal. However, the inexperienced ones were to be pitied most because they still saw those fast-talking swindlers and cocksure scoundrels as heroes and saviors. The bait-and-switch hadn't kicked in.

It was always the same. A man applied high pressure tactics for womanly flesh he felt entitled to and, before she could sleep on it, a naked woman shook under the temporary warmth of an emergency blanket. Somehow she'd paid a painful debt she didn't owe. From there, her path diverged: she either regained control through the use of her body and sexuality, or surrendered to victim status. When it came down to essentials, the man's motives closely resembled that of a pimp or a john. If only each woman felt her worth; there wouldn't be an imbalance of power.

Many had succumbed to Stockholm syndrome. Leah knew they'd turn on her if she spoke up on their behalf. After all, no one had ever requested an advocate. Nor had they indicated the desire to have a third party dive in and rescue them. In their minds, the abuses were a romantic subplot in a prime time episode about hardship and adversity. Sure, each woman wished for better but she wasn't in a position to ruin what might be the best role to ever come along. Happily ever after was *para mañana*[1]. She had to strategize for survival today.

Leah didn't have the right to expose anything against

their express wishes. Besides, what could she do? Broadcast the tamer sins of Prince Auto Plaza over loudspeakers and pray for the best?

She thought she heard the paging system pick up. A game show host's voice made the following pronouncements, accompanied by canned audience responses:

"Donald the Gambler. The guy who keeps buying lunch for the Redhead so maybe she'll let you touch her no-no zone one day. C'mon, she's had four abortions. Give her a break."

"Tommy Prince. The narcissist who bruised every girlfriend he ever had. There's a reporter on line one."

"Henry Martin, aka Wet Willy. Stop sniffing around Leah Owers and asking about her undergarments. Your wife is waiting on line two."

"Moose Stalwart. Did you know your stripper girlfriend and your common law wife have the same chatty gynecologist? Please call the Luxury Manager."

"Aldo the drug dealer. Thanks for pouring tequila shots during end-of-month close for female employees who would take off their tops for you. By the way: Are the young girls who visit you at work over eighteen? El Paso P.D. is on line three."

"Will Housely. Your porn video collection has expanded to include gay titles. Does that mean you're bisexual? If so, call Yermo's extension."

"Top Dog Bobby Dean. When you took your fiancé to Housely's Halloween party last year, why didn't you leave when your boss opened his bath robe and exposed his ding-dong? Your manhood is waiting on line four."

"Mo and Abe. You both have to take a comprehensive paternity test because she doesn't know which one of you got her pregnant. Call the title clerk immediately."

"Joey the Service Manager. Your baby momma is depressed because she didn't know about your record. Statutory rape of a fourteen-year-old? Good luck being a dad, when you aren't permitted near schools, daycares, and parks. Hope you warn your daughter about losers like yourself."

"Frank Villanueva. You proposed a threesome with the cashier when you were married, and you claim your ex-wife had problems."

"Chen. You're paying child support to you-know-who and now you're in arrears to your ex-wife. Might want to approach your loan shark friend for a cash advance. Please stop playing Black Jack at the casino, and call the attorney general's office."

"Mario. Your girlfriend knows you slept with her sister. Tell your Chihuahua brother Rogelio to watch your back, especially late at night after work."

"Rogelio. Mario's girlfriend will never have a reason to tell him she slept with you. Rest easy, brother."

"Ronnie. You showed the guys those photos you took of the bare naked Supermodel when she was passed out drunk last weekend. Why did you trick her? Why did you laugh behind her back? Your conscience is waiting on line five."

"Arturo. She doesn't want to listen to how you watch people through ceiling tile security mirrors. By the way: When was the last time you washed your hands?"

Game show theme music and applause noise ended with a satisfying click.

Leah groaned. Housely's headphones represented the fact that every offense was already on the record, but it didn't make any difference. Nothing had changed, and nothing would. At least, not while the powers-that-be remained on their lofty pedestals. That wasn't pessimism or lack of faith on her part; that was reality.

There must be something more I can do.

---

1. *para mañana*
    For tomorrow. (Spanish)

EIGHTEEN

Unnecessary Roughness

Leah walked in early after two days off. She felt restored and had an intense determination to make things happen. Nothing would steal her joy. She had a fresh mindset, and a new plan with five mileposts:

- Reestablish herself as a hard worker.
- Have the audacity to reach for more.
- Earn and receive a promotion.
- Rise above middle management degenerates, with the aim to secure her own automotive franchise.
- Secure a dealership within ten years.

There wasn't anything she couldn't do. Limitations were self-imposed, and she refused to underestimate herself. However, she knew she couldn't anticipate every move the opposition might make, so she prayed for perspective and a champion. She needed someone with know-how to guide her on the blessed road to ownership.

She knocked on Gerald's door to check the status of a credit application. When it opened, she saw all the Sales and Finance Managers crammed into the large office. She'd forgotten it was one of the Save-A-Deal mornings. The meetings were management only and they didn't like to be disturbed. She apologized for the interruption. Gerald waved her inside.

"That's alright. Why don't you tell us what you think?"

She heard the door click shut behind her.

Erik had a dumb smile on his face. He held out a large black dildo. She was unnerved, and it showed. The room laughed.

"Touch it," Wet Willy dared.

She shot him a warning look.

"We're just setting up a prank," Erik soothed. There was a ruddiness to his nose and cheeks. She'd noticed he was constantly in some stage of intoxication lately.

"Frank is on vacation this week. Later, probably after we close the month, Gerald is going to show me how to take apart Frank's chair, remove some of the filling to hide this in there, and put it back together so he doesn't notice the difference. It's a vibrator, with a battery-operated remote control. He won't know until it's too late."

"Gerald used to work in his uncle's upholstery shop," Housely explained.

Stalwart and the rest of the Managers gave their full attention to the Machiavellian conspiracy. She noted the Supermodel was absent.

"Leah should take the first test drive[1]," Wet Willy instigated.

"Unnecessary roughness. Fifteen yards, first down."

They seemed amused by her attempt to speak their language.

"Did you get credit approval for the Petersons yet?"

"That one signed last night," Aldo confirmed. "Silke's customer."

She opened the door.

"Correction. Silke's half-deal, because I was out sick. Erik, I hope Frank feels the love."

Raucous laughter ensued.

SHE COMPLETED a few tasks before she went to her desk. The pride of Prince Auto Plaza ended their meeting and spilled out into the showroom floor. At that very moment, the Advertising Manager and her camera guy arrived. They began to set up a TV commercial shoot for Tommy Prince. Melanie wore a black and white leopard print dress. Coupled with her angular features, the dress gave her the appearance of a cartoon villainess who coveted a Dalmatian skin coat. Leah exulted at the sight.

She dialed the youngest clerk downstairs and asked for a favor.

After she returned the phone to its cradle, Leah caught Erik and made another request. He told her it would cost eight burritos from the roach coach[2] on Saturday morning. Four *picadillo*[3], and four *machaca con frijoles y queso*[4]. She acted like the price was steep, but agreed to his terms anyway. They settled it with a handshake.

She sat behind her desk and applied eyeliner as she waited for the next stage of her plot to kick into gear.

ARTURO, a recent hire, wandered in for his sales shift. The guy had been a grocery store assistant Manager, and he claimed to moonlight as a private chef for parties and events. He was about thirty years old and had a crumpled appearance. Leah couldn't fathom sampling any morsel those fingers prepared. He recovered his messages from the reception area and disappeared into a cubicle. Less than five minutes later, Arturo sat across her desk. He didn't mention the clerk who passed the message to him. Instead, he started on a rant about Housely.

"I can't believe I have to work for that rat-face mother."

"What's your issue?"

She subtly glanced in Housely's direction. He was in the sales tower[5].

"William Housely is a crook."

"Oh yeah?"

"My dad was a fifth circuit court judge. He reviewed his federal case."

"What was his crime?"

"He ran a floor plan scam at his own dealership. He had a jet and everything."

Leah knew that was not what she wanted to discuss. She grabbed the reigns and steered him toward another topic.

"Why did you come here?"

"The potential income stream. My dad helped me get the job."

"No. Why are you here? At my desk?"

"Oh, a birdie told me you want to hear my story about ceiling mirrors."

She looked at him with disdain.

"Quite the contrary. You're at my desk to hear what I have to say."

"O-kay."

"When we're done here, you'll receive an exclusive invitation."

That piqued his interest.

"But only if you prove yourself worthy."

"What do you wanna chat about?"

"No talky-talky. Listen and receive. Understand?"

He responded with an excessive number of nods.

"You get off when you can look down at others. Have you read about the temptation of a rabbi the western world calls Jesus Christ?"

Leah kept up the charade for several minutes. She said The Devil entices man the same way he tried to recruit *Yeshua*[6]. Hunger, thirst, and other physical frailties were primary. The other temptations were presented from an apex: Soar off the pinnacle of the temple because you're invincible; Kneel before me on the high mountain, and I'll give you dominion over everything you see.

She made it up on the fly based on what she'd read. Then she added some tidbits about Asherah poles and high places, which indicated sites of pagan worship and prostitution. She reflected on the symbolism of the pole and implied it represented a phallus in some cultures. Although she ultimately meant to feed Arturo a bunch of nonsense, she couldn't help but to mix in historical fact and make it more believable.

"Do you see that woman over there?"

She pointed a steady finger at Melanie, the Advertising Manager, who was finished with Tommy's close-up. Melanie touched Tommy's arm, tossed her hair back, and cackled. The woman seemed to have a flair for the melodramatic. Arturo craned his head to look at her.

Leah embellished upon the Prince dynasty; they'd been aligned with the occult for several generations. The dealership existed solely for appearances, and there was a hidden layer to the organization. It consisted of men at every level who were handpicked to participate in secret rites. The

Devil himself, she asserted, possessed the unclothed body of Melanie the Advertising Manager on one unholy night every year. In exchange for twelve lunar cycles of prosperity and virility, the invited newcomer would ceremoniously disrobe before her and bow low. Then he'd receive his unjust reward.

"Do you want exceeding prosperity? Unquenchable virility?"

Arturo slowly nodded his head. There appeared to be a tad bit of hesitation, a healthy form of caution, in his demeanor. She didn't think it was skepticism though. At least she hoped it wasn't, so her plan would succeed.

She finalized her sermon with simple but very specific instructions. To opt into the unholy alliance, he must visit Erik at the Truck Center and utter the archaic phrase *carpe gallus*[7]. Nothing more, nothing less. If he met with Erik's approval, Arturo would get a preview of the mysterious, unjust reward all newcomers received from a dark, powerful force at the ceremony. Instructions would follow. She stood to indicate their meeting was over and dismissed him with a flick of her hand.

He exited the building and immediately went in the direction of the Truck Center. She called Erik's extension to give him a heads up. In less than ten minutes, Arturo returned with Erik and followed the much taller man like a puppy. They turned and went through the finance hallway. Erik didn't as much as glance in Leah's direction. She went over to the reception desk and braced for fireworks.

Within moments, there was a shout from Gerald's office. Arturo scurried out, practically on all fours like a bad dog. He was alabaster. His eyes were wide with peril. Erik followed him with a steady gait. Arturo arched his back to avoid an imaginary touch from behind.

Erik's monophonic bass voice chanted in Latin gibberish. His arms reached toward the smaller man, a rubbery phallus clenched in his left palm. He didn't drop the character until he came to the end of the hallway.

Arturo did a squeaky slide several feet to home base, grabbed his car keys, and ducked out a side door. That's when Erik finally made eye contact with Leah. He gave her a knowing wink and strutted back to the Finance Director's office.

Leah closed her eyes and quietly laughed to herself. She made a mental note to sneak Arturo's mailing address from the payroll clerk. In a few days, a leather bound book would arrive from an anonymous sender. He might find its redemption story beneficial.

Surprisingly, only two or three salespersons noticed the hullabaloo. Valerie answered an incoming call and forwarded the line so she could go to the restroom. Housely and Stalwart were engrossed in car deals. Others directed their attention to the famous Tommy Prince, even though his commercial shoot was no longer in progress. The dealer principal and Melanie were engaged in conversation on the portico outside, next to a few smokers. The camera guy dismantled the lighting equipment.

There was no one, other than Leah, in that area of the showroom floor. Without warning, a hot vapor defied her personal space.

"Get out!" snarled an unrecognizable, effeminate voice into her face.

She jerked her head back. Her chest burned with a flame of authority that spread to her fingertips. Static electricity raised the hairs on top of her head.

"You don't tell me what to do."

The cloud recoiled and dissipated into hisses.

<hr>

1. test drive

   Driving of a motor vehicle to determine its drivability or road-worthiness, and general operating state.

2. roach coach

   A blue collar catering truck.

3. *picadillo*

   Description of a burrito filled with lean ground beef, tomato, potatoes, and spice. (Spanish)

4. *machaca con frijoles y queso*

   Description of a burrito filled with marinated skirt steak, onions, peppers, tomatoes, and chilis. Topped with beans and cheese. (Spanish)

5. sales tower

   Term used to describe where the sales managers sit when penciling deals.

6. *Yeshua*

   The name of a beloved rabbi born approximately two millennia after Abram son of Terah. Crucified by Roman soldiers and died on a hill the same moment the Passover lamb was killed for Temple sacrifice. Literally, "salvation." (Hebrew)

7. *carpe gallus*

   Seize the rooster or cock. (Latin)

NINETEEN

Factions

Leah watched a turf war develop between Silke and Donald the Gambler based on Prince Auto's frequent payment of one hundred dollar bird-dogs[1]. Those incentives prompted Silke's boyfriend to bring referrals from Fort Bliss all the time. Some were soldiers from his unit, and others he met on or off post. He handed over to her any fees he was paid, and she thanked him in other ways.

Donald spent hard-earned money to advertise in a Fort Bliss print publication to target active duty members of the military. He also used his own funds to set up a site on the Internet. Ten or fifteen prospects filled out a contact form every week. He worked those leads until he was able to schedule sales appointments. When he ultimately sold a prospect, he'd offer to pay them one hundred dollars for a referral.

It wasn't long before a problem arose. One evening, Silke's boyfriend brought someone to the showroom with the same name and phone number as one of Dan's prospects. Both Silke and Donald claimed the customer. They fought like cats and dogs to avoid a split[2] deal.

The reason he knew about Silke's prospect in the first place was that sales consultants had to log their ups and be-backs on the showroom traffic log by the sales tower[3]. Mr. Jameson told Leah that was a rookie mistake. Green peas always logged accurate contact information. Veteran sales consultants were wise to the fact they should disguise their customer's info with a misspelled name or a wrong phone number. The info on the sheet could be used by unscrupulous salesmen, like Yermo, to skate[4] each other or claim a fictional connection to a customer for an undeserved half-deal.

Silke went on the defense after that and didn't provide truthful contact details anymore. Donald continued to hunt down every scrap of information he could find about her sold and unsold customers, especially if someone showed up in a military uniform. That provoked Silke to go on the offense. She began to aggressively skate him in return. It was never-ending, and cutthroat. Managers tried not to pull their own hair out as they refereed the fights, but they were thrilled by the increase in business.

Leah couldn't see the strings but, after her encounter in the showroom, she became hypersensitive to the horizontal control bar below. Oh, how she wanted to bewilder the marionettists who yanked at will but Holy Script made no mention of transcendent shears.

Or how to procure such a pair.

HER PHONE CUSTOMER WAS IRATE.

"It's the same car!"

"Sir, it can't be. The manufacturer rolled out hundreds of cars identical to it. They're all over the nation."

"I'm not stupid. I checked the VIN."

Leah froze. *How is that possible?*

"Sir, I don't know what to say. There must be some mistake."

"Are you saying two cars can have the same 17-digits?"

"No, I—."

"You lied to me."

His assertion disturbed her, and she was determined to investigate.

LEAH AND BEKA went for a Sunday afternoon cruise in Mommy's car. They arrived at Molek Motors, an independent car lot on the Montana motor mile. It was the place where her aggravated customer claimed to have found and purchased a car identical to the one Prince Auto had in stock a month earlier. He said Molek's price was two thousand dollars less than Prince's price. The place appeared to be open for business.

She browsed with Beka on her hip. The tiny, white portable building displayed banners that read, Buy Here Pay Here, *Se Habla Español*[5], and Bad Credit No Problem. There were between fifty to sixty vehicles in stock, mostly five years old or newer. She walked up to a magenta 2-door coupe. It had a business card stuck in the driver side window.

"Ibrahim Rahmani," she read. The hairs on the back of her neck bristled. That was the full name of Abe, one of the Camel Jockeys at Prince Auto.

"*Buenos tardes*[6]," an older Hispanic man greeted from the doorway.

"Hi," she responded. "*Habla usted inglés*[7]?"

He nodded.

"I apologize, I might be at the wrong place. Who is the owner of Molek Motors?"

"Abe Rahmani," he answered.

"Abe," she replied. "Does he have a son?"

"No, no children. Young man. He not married."

She appreciated the man's willingness to speak English to make things easier for her, even if he spoke in broken English.

"Do you know Mo Rahmani?"

He nodded.

"*Ellos son hermanos*[8]."

She stared at him. He'd just described Mo and Abe.

"You like talk? He come back five minute."

"No, not today. *Muchas gracias*[9]."

Her mind sounded an alarm to flee the scene of the crime. She wasn't certain what The Camel Jockey twins were up to, but she didn't want to be guilty by association.

Beka whimpered and blabbed in baby speak.

"Don't worry. Mommy knows."

They both sensed it.

---

1. bird-dog

    A fee paid for a customer referral.

2. split

    A term used to describe when the commission on a car deal is divided up between two salespeople.

3. sales tower

    Term used to describe where the sales managers sit when penciling deals.

4. skate

    A term used to describe when a customer is stolen from another salesperson.

5. *Se Habla Español*

    Spanish is spoken. (Spanish)

6. *Buenos tardes*
   Good afternoon. (Spanish)
7. *Habla usted inglés*
   Do you speak English? (Spanish)
8. *Ellos son hermanos*
   They are brothers. (Spanish)
9. *Muchas gracias*
   Thank you very much. (Spanish)

TWENTY

Men Who Misbehave

Another end-of-month close. Leah's next check was going to be a healthy one, and she was relieved. Her Sunday prospects still worked out well, but it was more difficult than ever to get units on the board and make a good month. She really had to hustle. The recent surges in sales hires expanded the team to almost twice their previous size. Management's decision caused an unintentional negative outcome because now each sales consultant had far fewer walk-in opportunities to work with.

The immediate answer Managers provided was that everyone needed to improve their closing ratios. However, that logic only went so far. Most of her sold customers were happy and satisfied, so she made sure always to request referrals. Some of the veteran salesmen paid cash to receptionists who transferred phone calls directly to their extensions. She thought she might need to resort to those methods soon.

There was no real need for Leah to be there after midnight, or even past 9 p.m. for that matter, but it was still an end of month requirement for sales and finance staff. A way the Managers forced the serfs to show their fealty. She had all her ducks in a row, per usual. No missing items for any of her car deals. She didn't look forward to another late night three-ring circus but, that time, it would provide necessary cover for a clandestine operation. She was on a mission.

Codename: No Fury Like A Woman Scorned.

Chelsea, the finance secretary, would do a process called billing to over a hundred car deals that evening. Most of those deals signed between midmonth through the day before but the Finance Managers and sales consultants didn't get missing paperwork, deposits, or addendums squared away until the very last day. She would separate paperwork into three packets: the dealership copy, the lender copy, and the Texas DMV[1] copy. Each packet had a copy of the driver's license. Once she finished with a stack of deal jackets[2], one of the Finance Managers would retrieve the stack from upstairs and place it in the ladies' office downstairs.

It was after hours now, so those employees were gone, but the next morning they'd come in and remove the packets. They'd file the dealership's copy and send the others to their destinations. On any other day of the month, each deal received a whole lot more scrutiny. However, it was the eve of a new fiscal month and too many deals were pushed through the pipeline in a hurry. Every deal that made it downstairs would go on the books and payroll would compensate sales consultants, Sales Managers, and Finance Managers in two business days. If, sometime later, they were to find anything important had been missed, they'd notify management with a red alert. The Managers, in turn, would hound the sales consultant to correct the error.

Leah's plot was inspired by a request Gerald once made of her. He'd given her a copy of a driver's license and told her to follow precise instructions: Go to the copier; set the toner settings to the lowest level; make a copy; then make another copy of that copy. She rolled her eyes when she deduced he wanted the lightest possible copy of the driver's license she could make. *What's with the mental handholding?* She didn't catechize him for it and just went about the rest of her day. It wasn't her customer anyway. Now, she'd apply a similar method to six of Skinny Carlos's car deals.

She walked downstairs under the guise of a restroom visit, since the one upstairs was under renovation. After she inserted the Dutch door's top and bottom latches, she double-checked each to make certain they weren't loose or faulty. Then she approached the stacks of deals that lined the top of a long filing cabinet.

The room smelled like dry erase markers and shampooed carpet. Her heart beat rapidly in her chest and she tried to steady her breaths. She selected six deal jackets that indicated Carlos's name on their file tabs. She set those aside and removed all three copies of driver's licenses from each jacket. They were easy to find, because Chelsea always put them at the back of each stapled packet. All Leah had to do was carefully tear away the last pages.

When she accomplished that, she set aside one copy of each license and pulled out an envelope from her pocket. It contained several paper squares: copies of a photo she'd cut out of a magazine from the customer waiting area. The German shepherd was a hero police dog that had reportedly tackled and held an alleged burglar's testicles in its teeth. The squares were the exact size of a Texas driver's license photo. She used tape to cover all the driver photos with dog photos, and snorted at the sight. Then she made lighter copies, and attached altered copies to the back of each deal packet with the aid of a heavy-duty stapler. After she was done, she returned everything back to its original place.

She shredded the extraneous paperwork and left.

SHE CHECKED HER WATCH. There were three more hours to go in the bureaucratic Hellhole, but she didn't want to spend all of it in her chair. The showroom smelled of Jim Beam and secondhand smoke that crept in through the open double glass doors. She decided to go for a walk.

Steady traffic sounds came from the main thoroughfare. Red brake lights lined up ten car lengths from the busy corner and drivers waited for their fortunes to turn. New and used cars on the lot gleamed as if it were noontide. Leah's mind wandered to thoughts of what she and Beka might do that Sunday. Then to the classes she'd enroll Beka in later. The red brick two-story house they'd live in. Trips to Europe and Asia. She wanted to see the White Cliffs of Dover, visit the Sistine Chapel, and ride a bicycle on The Great Wall of China. Then, of course, there were all those diving spots and beaches. She'd want to cross a vast ocean in a vessel one day, but she'd save that for when she was old and wrinkled.

Her mind returned to her job. If only she were in charge of Prince Auto Plaza, what she'd change in a matter of a few short weeks. Part of her knew she'd never rest if she were an owner operator. Yet, she was willing to exchange leisure for soul satisfying work. As dealership principal, she'd have the chance to employ hundreds of people. She could provide a scholarship fund for their families. She and Beka would anonymously donate to local charities. They'd still be able to take fun trips together; Tommy always managed to find time for those. She'd encourage Beka to be involved in the family business.

Of course, she wouldn't want her daughter to be in a dealership like that. Women weren't respected, and trouble lurked around every corner. The General Manager and at least one more employee were alleged felons. Private conversations were recorded. Managers embezzled company funds. There was a blatant insurance scam, but no one batted an eyelash.

Then there were the white lies the dealership told lenders. Gerald often put a straw buyer on financed deals. That meant the primary signer never planned to drive the car. The actual driver was a relative or a friend who either wasn't creditworthy, or wanted a lower interest rate than his credit rating would allow. It was fraud, which was against the law.

She rarely saw Mo and Abe anymore. They were probably at their surreptitious shell game full time. Something was sketchy about Housely's briefcase and his advertising refunds, too. She couldn't quite put her finger on what it was.

LEAH WALKED BACK INSIDE. She'd noticed another briefcase also made frequent appearances. Once or twice every week, a different sorority girl would come by Aldo's desk. There were about three or four doppelgangers on rotation. Each had straight hair, clear skin, false lashes, and a tiny waist. They often wore Greek letters. During the young lady's visit, she'd either pick up or drop off a small metallic case that had a combination lock.

Everyone seemed to believe Aldo had many girlfriends;

no one cared if they were a decade or more too young for him. Leah didn't think she could say anything anyway because they appeared to be the age of consent. Still, she was overwrought because there was a rumor Aldo had ties to the cartel. He probably wasn't anything more than a small-time drug dealer, but there was a chance his *chiquis*[3] on that side of the border could get mixed up with hardened criminals.

She knew several other employees also had contacts in the underworld. There was the Elvis impersonator. His big bouffant bled black hair coloring, and he claimed he wasn't in the witness protection program. He swore he'd grown up in the southwest and his grandparents were from Mexico, although he didn't understand much, if any, Spanish. Instead, he called a cheese pizza a "plain pie" in a distinctly New Jersey accent. He refused to sit with his back to an exit, and seemed overly wary of his surroundings. Also, Donald the Gambler was chased down by thugs a few times when he owed money to his sports bookie. He couldn't get any help from Carlos the Loan Shark. He was denied a line of credit. Then there was the sales consultant who sold fake ID cards. He said he'd pay twenty bucks for private customer info, but Leah pretended not to hear.

Many male employees didn't need the underworld; they misbehaved badly without much assistance. Leah overheard one sales consultant talk about how he supported two wives and two sets of children. He had one family on each side of the border. Leah was sure that meant he was a bigamist, but she wasn't entirely sure how international law treated that kind of situation. A veteran sales consultant had a young bride who used to be his kids' babysitter. His new wife didn't know how to access any of the bank accounts. Every payday, she came by the showroom for her allowance. He'd make her sit across his desk and count out the stack of twenties at his desk, most of which would go to groceries or other household needs. All the other salesmen envied him. Leah overheard another salesman over forty complain he had to pay a *señorita*[4] to cook and clean whenever his wife went on an annual getaway with her gal pal.

Early on, Aldo the drug dealer asked Ronnie if her mosquito bites itched. In retaliation, she placed a gallon jar labeled Veronica's Boob Job in the sales tower[5]—and it was still there. Every so often, she solicited a Manager for a contribution. Her goal was to raise cash for breast augmentation surgery in Mexico. To Leah, that seemed to highly motivate Sales and Finance Managers to put together more deals for her. Even when her car deal seemed impossible, they'd find a way.

Leah's thoughts returned to Donald the Gambler as she watched him mindlessly shuffle a deck of playing cards at his desk while he talked on the phone. He was a charming, likeable guy in general. He loved to show card tricks to customers' kids. Leah was disappointed he couldn't stop Chen's wager. Several male employees had placed bets about how many lunches it would take for him to bed the Redhead. Donald pursued the young receptionist with a passion. To date, the count was at six and holding.

"Leah Owers, to the finance office," someone paged.

She wondered what that could be about. In the finance hallway, she looked to her left and to her right. Aldo signed two retirees she didn't recognize. Henry Martin was not in his office. The lights to the Supermodel's office were off because she'd cut her losses and run. Leah knocked on Gerald's door. Henry, Mr. Wet Willy himself, opened it with glee. She sighed out of frustration and went in, and he closed the door behind her.

Erik and Gerald were diligently at work on their mischievous side project. They sat by the window.

"Did you need me?" she asked the two.

Erik shrugged. Gerald concentrated on the task before him.

She faced Henry, who had apparently summoned her. Lately, his capricious nature fluctuated between impulsive frat boy and distinguished gentleman. His height and facial features made it possible to pull off the latter. However, when customers weren't around, he'd often hop around like an energized Easter bunny. Maybe he was on drugs. His unpredictable mood swings irritated her. She almost wished he'd just be a clumsy sexual harasser again.

Before she could stop him, he seized her waistband with one hand and the midsection between underwire cups with his other. In one swift motion, he utilized the makeshift handles to powerlift her body high above his head. She was frightened by the sudden, raw display of strength. Her legs kicked and her arms flailed helplessly as she tried to swim out of the room. With all the exertion, it felt as if her tampon might slide out.

Oh no, please. Don't let them see me bleed.

Heat rushed into her face. Pain seared from her sternum to her ovaries. Tears sprang from her eyeballs but words wouldn't come. She couldn't breathe, and panicked. She slapped at Henry's head but it was out of reach. Black edges of the room grew thick. Her strength waned. As her last will and testament, she tapped out a distress signal on the moron's forearm. One-two-three. One. Two. Three. One-two-three.

He almost dropped her on the carpet. She doubled over, coughed, and gasped loudly for air. The sight of her paralyzed the other two men. Henry laughed like a tickle torturer after an especially productive session. She wiped away black mascara streaks with white tissue from the box on Gerald's desk.

A minute passed before her breaths normalized. She timidly straightened her posture because her right nipple was caught in her bra's twisted fabric and she was unsure about where her left breast was headed. Something also had to be done about the throbbing discomfort between her uterus and vagina, at least before her pants caught the brunt of it. Things could get messy real fast but, first, she had to confront the adolescent's physical assault.

"Take your foreplay upstairs," Gerald said.

She took a sharp breath.

Erik avoided eye contact.

Wet Willy reached for her shoulder but she whirled away from him and let the door pummel the office wall in her wake. He vocalized surprise at her emotional instability.

The only place she wanted to be right then was behind a locked ladies' room door. That wasn't an auto plaza, that place was Hell.

---

1. DMV

    Department of Motor Vehicles.
2. deal jacket

    A folder that contains all the information in a customer's transaction.
3. *chiqui*

    A common nickname that could mean several things including shorty, cutie, or little girl. (Spanish)
4. *señorita*

    An unmarried woman. (Spanish)
5. sales tower

    Term used to describe where the sales managers sit when penciling deals.

Hell Felt Tremors

A few days later, Leah leaped over steam-filled asphalt cracks to sell cars. She maintained a safe distance from lava that flowed out of the F&I[1] hallway as various lenders and the DMV[2] kicked back Hell's Auto Plaza submissions with invalid driver's licenses. When the finance secretary and the title clerk discovered the pattern of German Shepherds, they searched dealership files together and were astonished to find the same copies in there. They immediately reported the irregularity to their supervisors, who notified Gerald.

All the problem car deals belonged to Skinny Carlos.

Sales and Finance Managers were inflamed. Someone's idea of a practical joke would delay funding for six vehicles that were over the curb[3]. In addition, customers wouldn't receive their license plates or windshield registration stickers in a timely manner. Much to Carlos's chagrin, Managers put him on notice. They raged at him that his employment status was at stake if he didn't fix it. He hurriedly called all six customers, tried to explain the gaffe, tracked down driver's licenses, and made copies. Two business days of a new month were squandered by last month's problems. From then on, he made extra copies for his personal records.

CARLOS MAY HAVE SEEN BETTER days, but Donald had a stroke of good luck. As the banalities Sales Managers reiterated day in and day out: The car business was a numbers game. The more attempts you made, the more deals you closed[4]. Call Until They Buy or Die[5]. No sooner was the upstairs ladies' restroom renovation completed than did the Gambler and the Redhead christen it on a lazy Tuesday afternoon. Leah saw them go in together and they didn't come out for at least ten minutes. Meanwhile, she stared sadly through a wall of showroom windows at the Franklin Mountains, reviewed her own past mistakes, and thought of Sammy with affection.

Not long after, Leah climbed the stairs by the finance hallway and returned a borrowed staple remover to Chelsea's desk. She intended to take the corridor to the desecrated ladies' room which the night crew had just cleaned up, but she stopped short. She could hear a fracas in one of the rooms. Sounds of labored breathing. A man's voice strained, as if he tried to move heavy furniture. An object hit a wall. Staccato cries in *sotto voce*[6].

She turned a one-eighty and did a Flo-Jo out of there. A few minutes later at her desk, she watched Stalwart walk downstairs and return to the sales tower[7]. Polyestrous queen cat Melanie followed shortly after and waved her lithe paw at the reception station. She rubbed herself against the tower's wooden panels, meowed at Housely, and high-tailed it out of the building to a yellow cab. Leah wondered what the General Manager would do to his Used Car Director, if he only knew.

The next day, Leah overheard a casual conversation between two lot attendants. Glass Eye told Hal that he'd heard a bump-bump-bump from inside the Truck Center. At first, he thought he should climb up on the roof and adjust the swamp cooler's belt tension. Then Frank and Ronnie came out of the recently renovated unisex bathroom, and the pesky noise stopped altogether. Leah wasn't surprised to hear that, but it made her even more concerned about Ronnie's proximity to Erik. Housely had approved Ronnie's recent transfer to the Truck Center and she worked late most nights.

Even when the Managers scheduled her for an earlier shift.

LEAH GAVE in and bought a cellular phone with a data plan. Aldo the drug dealer was first to get one. After other Managers saw his, they followed suit. They reasoned that every sales professional should be reachable in the event a customer had an emergency while they were out of the office. She thought it would come in handy for both business and personal use. Susie might want to share news about Beka's first word, or request more diapers from the store. The black Motorola flip phone reminded her of *Star Trek* communicators. In the seventies, the children in her neighborhood glued Tic Tac boxes to cereal box tops for hours of sci-fi fun.

On a drizzly Sunday morning, she parked her car in front of the dealership as a week's worth of volcanic ash washed away. She didn't think any prospects would show in that kind of weather, but it might clear soon. Her new phone rang, and she sparkled.

"It's me, Al."

She didn't get a chance to respond before the drug dealer continued.

"I want you to do me a favor. Don't worry, I'll take care of you."

Aldo recounted the return to his apartment about 3 a.m. only to find it ransacked. He was sure his jealous ex-girlfriend did it because "Die, *puto*[8]!" was written in lipstick on the bathroom mirror. He lamented the loss of all his precious worldly possessions. Leah suspected he'd later fill out an insurance claim with the description he gave. Price-less artifacts shattered to pieces. Expensive modern art paintings and a red chaise lounge, slashed with a pair of scissors. All the candles melted in the middle of his charred California king mattress. It was going to take him days to clean up the mess and move back in with his parents.

At the conclusion of their conversation, he explained that Tommy Prince placed weekly advertisements in the Sunday paper for his new Special Finance assistance program. When prospects dialed the toll-free 800 number, it would ring directly to a second phone in Aldo's office. He told her those customers were all cockroaches[9], but Tommy insisted the hotline be answered during normal business hours.

"All you have to do is answer those phone calls for me."

He told her to have a stack of credit applications ready so she could fill out a five-liner. She could sit in his office, or transfer the calls to her cell phone when she needed to do something else, but she must answer in a business-like manner before the second ring.

"Like I said, I'll take care of you. Do we have an understanding?"

"I'll do it on one condition: I'm the assigned salesperson."

"You got it, *chiqui*[10]!" he vowed.

LEAH WENT into Monday morning like gangbusters. She juggled multiple phone calls like a switchboard operator. Aldo had suggested she fill out a five-liner, but she called the prospects back for the rest of the information when the phones were dead. She also wanted to know what type of vehicle they sought: 2-door or 4-door, automatic or manual, light or dark colors, and number of passengers.

She asked Housely to pull the credit bureaus. He showed her when the consumer had a recent bankruptcy ruling or a repossession, and she put those applications in the temporarily dead stack. She retrieved a binder of current subprime credit programs from Aldo's desk drawer and poured through the pages. It helped her to determine which of the credit applicants had the best chance for approval. Housely also taught her how to calculate the debt-to-income ratio, and payment-to-income ratio.

Stalwart suggested several stock numbers that were "back of book." She went to the lot to examine each used vehicle, and then called her viable Special Finance prospects to schedule their test drive[11] appointments. By noon, she'd received positive bank callbacks for fifteen prospects. She prepared a deal jacket[12] for each one and repeated the process every time the hotline phone rang.

Her stomach rumbled for food. She debated pick up or delivery.

"Hello, Leah," said Tommy Prince.

Her back had been to the open doorway. She spun around in Aldo's chair to face the dealer principal.

"Hello! Those new bathrooms look better than I'd hoped. Thanks for doing that."

"I'm pleased with the results. Jake will have to update the men's." He gave her an appraising look. "I listened to your last phone conversation."

She could feel the heat rise into her cheeks. If Aldo got into trouble, all bets were off.

"Aldo wanted to take care of his customers, but he had an emergency."

"How did the call go?"

"That customer had a repo six months ago, but we have fifteen solid prospects from this morning. I've scheduled all of them for a test drive appointment."

She pointed to the stack of deal jackets.

Tommy looked startled.

"Come again? How many did you say?"

ALDO CALLED the Special Finance phone late in the afternoon to check on her. She reassured him that he didn't have anything to worry about. He asked if she'd seen Tommy in the building. Another line lit up, so she told him she had to go.

"Prince Auto Plaza's Credit Hotline."

"Hey, Rain Man!" shouted Henry across the hall.

Leah looked up and saw Timothy wander into Henry's office. She thought he might be lost, so she stood to get a better view.

He saw her through the glass windows and waved. She smiled and waved back.

"They put the wrong number on my check." He held what looked like a pay stub.

Leah apologized to the customer on the phone and got

his number so she could call him back. Then she crossed the hall into Henry's office to help.

"Do you need to see payroll? They're down the stairs by the service drive. Want me to show you?"

"Hey. We're having a talk here, mano a mano. Give us a moment."

Leah stepped away but didn't leave.

The older man sat in his chair and ordered Timothy to sit on the edge of his desk. When he was situated, they had a shallow discussion about luxury imports.

Henry queried if he had a girlfriend. He blushed and said maybe Leah would be his girlfriend, but he didn't know yet.

Henry told him to remove his foam earphones because it wasn't polite.

"Besides, don't you think that's a baby habit?"

He reluctantly obeyed the Manager.

Henry winked at Leah over his reading glasses and her stomach recoiled. She thought she might need to vomit.

Henry took out his wallet and showed off photos of his wife and children. While he artfully distracted Timothy with the family photos, he slyly stuck a finger into his mouth. Leah had seen him do the same thing before.

In the vice-principal's office. When hairy knuckles dragged across her inner thighs.

Wait. What?

Her nerve endings lit on fire.

Without hesitation, the heel of her palm repulsed opposite electromagnetic energy and slammed it into Henry's nose. His glasses flew into the window blinds. Blood trickled from his nostrils and he tried to stop the stream with his bare hands.

The tense muscles in her throat ached like she wanted to cry, but she didn't.

She tossed Henry's wallet on his desk and guided Timothy through the doorway.

The young man gingerly placed the foam earphones back over his ears.

"You know, I think the office ladies have leftover birthday cake."

"I hope they have chocolate."

She put her arm around him and patted his shoulder. Emotions made it difficult to swallow, let alone speak above a whisper.

"Me too."

They didn't take a backward glance.

"LEAH OWERS. CALL THE OPERATOR."

Leah dialed zero and waited for Valerie to pick up.

"Hello, Miss Owers. Mr. Prince wants you to come to his office."

"Now?" she fretted.

"Yes, he said right away."

---

1. F&I
    An acronym for Finance and Insurance.
2. DMV
    Department of Motor Vehicles.
3. over the curb
    A sales transaction that has been completed and the customer has driven the vehicle off the lot.
4. close
    Term to describe the act of convincing a customer to agree to a sales transaction.
5. Call Until They Buy or Die
    An old saying from management to salespeople.
6. *sotto voce*
    Sung or said in a quiet voice, as if not to be overheard. (Italian)
7. sales tower

Term used to describe where the sales managers sit when penciling deals.

8. *puto*

An insult to anyone perceived to be weak or contemptible. Also an expletive. (Spanish)

9. cockroach

Slang term used by old school salespeople to refer to bad credit customers who they feel are wasting their time.

10. *chiqui*

A common nickname that could mean several things including shorty, cutie, or little girl. (Spanish)

11. test drive

Driving of a motor vehicle to determine its drivability or road-worthiness, and general operating state.

12. deal jacket

A folder that contains all the information in a customer's transaction.

TWENTY-TWO

An Offer He Couldn't Refuse

Leah looked over at Henry's vacant office. He had the misfortune of a nosebleed, and went to change into a clean shirt. As she climbed the stairs, she felt as if her head were on the chopping block.

When she went into Tommy Prince's office, he presented her with a pay plan that included a base salary with a performance incentive. She was promoted to Special Finance Manager. Tommy said Aldo would continue as F&I[1] Manager but he'd be free from the hassle of the credit hotline.

She'd be assigned a desk in a different location, yet to be determined. She'd direct all Special Finance leads from start to finish. Housely would instruct her how to desk deals on the DMS[2]. Finance Managers would teach her how to print contracts and title documents. She'd have sole responsibility for her deals, and must ensure banks funded them within ten days. Tommy expected to see a full report on his desk after every end-of-month close.

Since Special Finance was Tommy's initiative, based on feedback from his 20 Group peers, Leah would answer directly to him. That confused her because, within the official organizational hierarchy, General Manager Will Housely had seniority over sales and finance. Tommy offered clarity: Although she'd cooperate with existing departments, she couldn't allow car business tradition to dominate in that new space. As she'd already discovered, Special Finance deals necessarily worked backwards from the normal car deal. Instead of an afterthought, lenders were brought to the table from the start. That single modification simplified an overly complex process and reduced customer friction. She agreed it made absolute sense.

Tommy incited high hopes; he told her to think of herself as captain of a separate ship. He'd provide general oversight but she'd set the course. For those reasons, she became enthusiastic and couldn't wait to roll out the red carpet for second chance finance customers.

She was already at milepost number three of her five-point plan.

WHILE LEAH and her customers were on the used car lot, she saw a young lady step out of the backseat of a yellow sports car and go into the building. She looked like one of Aldo's many sorority doppelgangers with her long, straight hair. However, this time, something was very different about the visit because the driver followed her inside. A few minutes later, a salesman opened the door for them. As expected, the smiling college girl held a metallic briefcase's handle with a death grip. Marvin the bachelor, from Randall Fenton's class, was right behind her. He wore aviator shades. In his arms were a small box of video cassettes. Leah's conversation stalled and she nearly went off the rails.

She stammered as her heart, soul, and strength struggled to get her mind off homicide and back on track.

TOMMY PRINCE WANTED Leah to go to dinner with an out-of-town visitor from the captive lender. It was the dealership's most important banking relationship, but he had a prior engagement he either couldn't, or wouldn't, cancel. Gerald would have been the natural first choice to go but he was apoplectic because he had to cover for his Finance Managers. They seemed to have dropped like flies.

The banker's name was Billy Bruce. He was a sanguine, middle age man with large jowls. Billy hailed from Nebraska. He'd been married for almost thirty years to his lifelong sweetheart. Their three teenagers were in high school and their two adult children were away at a university. He was the Southwest representative and would be in the area for a couple more days. Leah agreed to meet him at a steakhouse by the airport.

She found him at the bar.

When he'd finished his Jack and Coke, the hostess seated them. Their waitress came by their table to take the order. Leah was in a celebratory mood but, even if she hadn't been, Billy had a buoyant personality that could lift anyone. He gave her his business card and asked lots of questions. He wanted to know about the path that led her into car sales and Special Finance. She gave him the highlights about the job ad, the interview, and the sales trainer. She told him the most joy in her work came when she could make things easy for customers.

"Basically, I was in the right place at the right time."

"Aww, now, I don't know about that. I'm positive you

were promoted because you did a great job and they saw potential."

"You know Will Housely, our GM?"

Their salads arrived. He requested another Jack and Coke.

"Will Housely?" A glimmer of recognition, but he shook his head.

"How long have you known Tommy Prince?"

"Let's see." His eyes drifted back through their business relationship. "I don't know him very well. I met his father, Tommy Prince Jr., twelve or thirteen years ago when he was more involved in the dealership. I talk mostly with F&I Directors. Gerald and I have known each other about five years. Tell him I was sorry he couldn't be here tonight."

He explained his employer, the captive lender, was the financial services branch of the OEM[3]. Theirs was a symbiotic relationship. The manufacturer relied on the franchise dealership to serve consumers directly. The franchise, in turn, relied on the lending arm for a revolving line of credit. The captive lender was far more than simply the financer of auto loans. That was just one slice of the pie.

Dealership operations required efficient cash flow from month to month. The biggest drain on any car dealership's capital was their retail inventory. Prince Auto Plaza had more than fifteen million dollars of vehicles that collected dust on any given day. To avoid an outflow of too much cash, they participated in a Dealership Floor Plan. Prince Auto paid interest to the captive lender every month for every new and used vehicle until it was sold and paid off. Every day a vehicle wasn't funded cost Prince Auto actual dollars and cents.

Billy indicated another refill was in order. As they cut into medium rare New York strip steaks, Leah asked if there were many female dealer principals. He told her he'd met several over the span of his twenty-year career. Most of them were wives or daughters of dealers who helped them get started in the business. He heard of one woman in another territory who rose through the ranks at a dealership and later signed up an investor when she wanted to buy the franchise. Billy informed Leah the OEM actively recruited minority and female dealer candidates. It wanted to mirror the marketplace. Candidates who passed all stages of dealer development could expect to receive a generous line of business credit. For most applicants, their main obstacle was to prove they had access to millions of dollars of unencumbered capital. The initial cash investment was a requirement for entry into the program.

Their conversation returned to the topic of Prince Auto Plaza. The captive lender planned to host a dealer conference on the west coast in a few months. Every U.S. franchise would be there. It was an exclusive event. The manufacturer spared no expense. Tommy showed his face every year, but he always failed to send his photo in advance. That resulted in an embarrassing empty box next to his name and bio. It was a poor reflection on Billy as the dealer representative; he couldn't allow Tommy to repeat it.

He urged Leah to do him a huge favor.

"Little boys respond to a swift kick in the ass, but mighty men require a different type of coaxing. Tommy should see two clear options in front of him. Behind door number one, he can take the easy road and send his headshot by the deadline. If he chooses door number two, he'll have to endure a truly painful experience. The blank box in front of his bio isn't a deterrent. He couldn't care less about that; he enjoys giving us the middle finger. What he needs to understand is this: the result of no action will be so distasteful that he should avoid it altogether."

Billy shared the contents of his proposal. Leah agreed wholeheartedly and planned to execute first thing in the morning. They shook on it with big smiles.

The waitress cleared their table and offered dessert. He looked to Leah, but she politely declined. He ordered another round. She mentioned that she'd have to leave in a few minutes. She talked about her daughter and some of her dreams. Billy listened intently and asked questions for clarification.

After a while, his speech slowed. Leah lost track of how many she'd seen him drink but then she recalled he was already at the bar when she arrived. He talked about his lovely wife, a homemaker. Earlier that year she refreshed her résumé and landed a full-time job. He felt betrayed, of course, because they'd covenanted years prior that he'd be the only earner in the family. That was why he was away fifty weeks every year, to provide a house in which he was only able to live in for thirty-six hours per week at the most. He said his wife was concerned because they paid tuition, room, and board for two undergraduates and there were three more in the pipeline. She didn't see how they'd manage without an extra income.

He wept when he told Leah of his beloved youngest boy. His son was a freshman in high school and played football. He wanted to go to every game but it wasn't possible with his tight travel schedule.

The check eventually came, and he paid with his corporate card. He left a cash tip and excused himself to go to the restroom. While he was away, Leah motioned for the waitress to come over and added ten dollars to the tip.

"He's staying at the Marriott. Don't let him drive."

When he returned, Leah thanked him for dinner. She said she'd be happy to give him a ride back to his hotel. He said he wanted to take a stroll, so she promised she'd call in the morning. After she talked to Tommy.

LEAH STOPPED in the dealer principal's open doorway and knocked.

"Come in." Tommy waved for her to enter and looked at his computer monitor.

"I can't stay, my customer is on her way. I just came to deliver a critical message from Billy Bruce."

"Alright."

Leah cleared her throat. She'd rehearsed her lines on the way to work.

"He needs your photo for the bio."

"That again?"

"Yes. Mr. Bruce said, if you don't mail your photo in an overnight package by 1 p.m. today, this is what he's going to do: He'll drive Montana Avenue and seek out the ugliest, toothless, homeless man he can find. He'll pay that individual twenty bucks for his photo. Then he'll mail that photo with your name attached."

Tommy looked at Leah's deadpan face and his jaw became unhinged. He sprang into action, picked up his cordless desk phone, and dialed a number.

He covered the receiver and asked her, "By what time?"

"Overnight it by 1 p.m., at the latest."

"Bring me a camera with a memory card, right now. I need to send a photo!"

Leah quietly withdrew.

Laughter bubbled up, but she bit her lip.

---

1. F&I

     An acronym for Finance and Insurance.
2. DMS

     Dealer Management System software.
3. OEM

     Original Equipment Manufacturer.

Orphans and Widows

H er work area would be set up at the Truck Center in a day or so. For now, she borrowed the office the Supermodel had vacated and forwarded hotline calls to her cell phone. Gerald didn't want Leah to move in permanently. He said that office was intended for F&I[1] Managers only and Special Finance wasn't part of F&I.

She brushed off that initial rejection until she received a cool reception from the rest of the management team. They didn't shun her; not exactly. She just didn't hear a single congratulations. Her promotion wasn't announced in a sales meeting. It was as if it had never happened. Tommy Prince wanted Car-Man the Magnificent to tutor her, but he refused to condescend to such an assignment. He delegated her DMS[2] lessons to Truck Center Managers.

Aldo snacked on *jalapeño*[3] nachos while he showed Leah how to use his finicky F&I dot matrix printer. She needed to insert documents at a slight angle so the print would be in alignment with the blanks on the page. It took several tries to come out right. She didn't understand why he didn't get the crooked mechanism repaired, and she prayed her F&I equipment would be in much better shape.

"Here's the document checklist," he said, and pulled a laminated paper from his files. "You know the front-end already, but you need to know the back-end too. Keep the original. I'm so busy when I sign a customer I go off memory. Chelsea usually lets me know if I forget something."

Well, that's stupid.

Leah willfully restrained her countenance and nodded politely. She made a mental note to use the finance checklist while customers were still in front of her. It would help to avoid a costly mistake, and banks would fund her deals quicker.

Aldo bit into another tortilla chip and cheese sauce dripped on his orange silk tie. He reached for a tissue but the box was empty. He grunted like an ape and searched his desk for a napkin substitute.

Cro-Magnon needs to evolve.

Silke barged into Aldo's office with Brittany in tow. She grabbed his Rolex and turned it toward her cohort.

"See? The second hand moves around the face in a smooth motion. It doesn't do that tick-tick-tick."

"Oh, I get it."

"So don't fall for those fakes no more."

"Let me see?" Leah asked. "Huh, I never knew about that."

"My best Christmas present ever. From Tommy."

"I think he should buy Leah one, too," Brittany said.

"*Jawohl*[4]! But why would he do that? Have you seen her rust bucket on wheels?"

Leah laughed hysterically at Silke's insult.

The two women backed away as if she'd exhibited a

venereal disease. They crossed the hall and embarked upon an inquisition into Henry's bruised eye sockets. He told them terrible allergies were the cause.

"One more thing."

Leah directed her attention back to Aldo.

"Staple checks to the front of the purchase order. When a customer gives you cash money, make sure you turn it in to the service cashier. Gerald had violent seizures last time I forgot."

She nodded again.

"Al, it's time," a woman's voice gently interrupted.

They looked up to see High-Bangs Betty with safety hazard eyeliner.

"Be right there."

He straightened the knot of his tie. The cheese stain was noticeable.

"That's all I've got for you. Good luck."

Aldo and Betty conferred in the hallway.

Leah thought it was strange the Comptroller would be involved in a drug test. Jan the Office Manager was the person who administered those, and only to new hires.

Nick, the luxury import salesman, soon joined in and they moved their huddle to the bottom of the stairs. The big guy lifted his pant leg. The other two examined the hairs while Betty explained something to Aldo. At last, the three seemed to reach an agreement and they went upstairs together.

SINCE LEAH WAS between phone calls and customer appointments, she called Flor at the body shop to discuss the congregation's annual fundraiser. Donations would benefit women and girls who escaped human trafficking.

Leah wanted to contact all her customers, many of whom were prominent members of the community or business owners, to recruit potential candidates for the fundraiser committee. Each member would be encouraged to sell tickets for as many tables as they could. She could host an informal brunch in the conference room and Flor could make a presentation. They talked about pamphlets and a Q&A. Flor wanted to wait until she got permission from her congregation, but she didn't think they'd have any problems with it.

Leah reached into her purse and pulled out her list of sold customers. As far as they'd be concerned, she was still their sales consultant. She might not want to tell them about her promotion. She'd wait to call until she could recruit for the fundraiser committee, of course, and then she'd give them her new phone number. They could call direct whenever they needed anything.

Her eyes scanned the list. The Farmer's phone number was in a different area code. He was not likely to drive so far for a fundraiser, but she could cheer him up with a call. She dialed the digits on her cell phone and waited.

"Y-ello?"

She smiled at the sound of his voice.

"Knock, knock," she proffered, as if she were the Queen of England.

"Who's there?"

"Orange."

"Orange who?"

She saw his crinkled-up nose in her mind's eye.

"Orange you glad I didn't say banana?"

He chortled.

It was silly, but she knew her audience.

"Miss Leah, is that you?"

She gave him the good news about her promotion. He

said he was proud she'd provide a second chance for those who'd messed up their credit the first time. His words encouraged her so much she wanted to segue to the fundraiser, but she wondered how to broach the subject of human trafficking with a gentleman of his generation. She chose to tell him only that she was involved with a congregation to help women and children get off the streets.

Before she could continue, he quoted a verse: "Seek justice for fatherless defendants and widowed plaintiffs."

He paused, and she could hear him breathe deeply.

"How much is a month's rent in El Paso?"

Leah remembered an ad for a one bedroom. The rent was seven hundred fifty. She described it to him.

Without further deliberation, he pledged to send a check for seven hundred fifty dollars. His generosity surprised her. She thanked him profusely, and he was somehow able to decipher the name of the non-profit organization through her sobs.

He promised to mail it in an envelope addressed to her name, care of Prince Auto.

After a few minutes, she needed to get back to work so they said goodbye.

SHE WAS haggard at sunset when it was time to move her car forward. Hal stopped by her desk to pick up the car keys. She was grateful but told him she'd feel more comfortable if she moved it herself every day. He relented and let her have her way.

As she walked to the parking garage between the front of the dealership and the employee parking lot, she saw a semi-circle formed by Housely, Stalwart, and Old Preacher

Johnson. Housely pointed what looked like a rifle at the concrete ceiling.

Pop! Pop! Two pigeons fell from the rafters. More air pops, and more carcasses.

She looked down and saw a fallen bird's nest.

It had eggs in it.

---

1. F&I

    An acronym for Finance and Insurance.

2. DMS

    Dealer Management System software.

3. *jalapeño*

    A very hot, green chili pepper used in Mexican-style cooking. (Spanish)

4. *Jawohl*

    Yes, absolutely. (German)

Secret Admirer

L eah drove the red custom-lifted truck through traffic. She liked how it felt to sit up higher than other vehicles, but the truck was only a loaner. Her Tempo was on standby for an oil change in the service department. The only opportunity she had to accomplish a little holiday shopping was between appointments. The mall closed most evenings before she left work. Other Managers also slipped out now and then to do the same.

As she waited for the light, her mind turned to a trip she might have to make. She'd overheard Housely and Gerald talk about a multi-day automotive conference scheduled for next quarter. Tommy wanted to send at least half the management staff that year. Whoever went would only stay for a day or two, to attend a couple of the sessions that pertained to their specific area of the dealership, and then they'd return. Gerald wanted to take at least one Finance Manager. Jan the Office Manager would make all the travel arrangements. She was likely to put Finance Managers in economy class. Leah pictured Gerald in first class while she jostled for elbowroom in the back of the plane.

The traffic light turned green. She proceeded a kilometer and then turned at the mall entrance. She wanted to get out of Hell Paso and see the car business from the corporate point of view. In addition, while she was there, she could network with her peers in other parts of the U.S. There was no way Gerald would miss out. He talked about last year's conference as if it had been a Mardi Gras parade.

She guessed it would be a fun trip unless she ended up next to Aldo. Somehow, he'd become convinced she snitched to Tommy about his abuse of illicit drugs. He had to fake his drug test with a hair sample from Nick the luxury import salesman. She figured Henry would avoid her like the plague if he went, which was completely fine with her. It was possible Housely and Gerald wouldn't want her to go at all, but she knew Tommy would overrule any adverse decisions. He encouraged and expected her participation.

There was an open parking spot near Dillard's. Leah seized the opportunity. She hopped out of the truck and walked to the entrance. She felt fancy because of a few new items she'd purchased on one of her previous shopping trips. A pink and white Ralph Lauren shirt with French cuffs. Mikimoto pearl earrings. A Dooney and Bourke purse that was on sale. Her glossy French tip manicure glinted in the sunlight and her hair was pinned up in a messy bun. There might be time to get a blowout at the salon.

Some of the women at work talked about special low rates for Botox treatments and Brazilian butt lifts. She wanted liposuction for her muffin top and love handles but she'd never go south of the border for that kind of procedure. It seemed too risky. A plastic surgeon on the west side quoted her five thousand dollars for lipo alone. She could put it on two or three credit cards. He said recovery would only take a few days…

WHEN SHE RETURNED to the dealership, she parked the loaner outside the Truck Center instead of in the used car lot. She might need it again later. The Credit Union would host a soirée at the El Paso Club that night and she was supposed to meet the Finance Managers there. She almost took her shopping bags inside but decided to leave them in the truck.

As she walked up the ramp, she noticed Frank and Mario on the lot with two customers in border patrol uniforms. Ronnie assisted three Mexican cowboys at the other end. Leah did a double take when she saw the pointy, elf-styled boots those men wore.

She opened the door and a strong aroma of chili cheese dogs with onion assaulted her nostrils. Rogelio sat at Erik's desk. They scarfed down the last few bites of their fast food lunch and discarded the trash.

"Guys, open a window."

She ignored the dozen sangria roses that arrived during her absence, and checked the fax machine for callbacks.

Erik retrieved a can of deodorizer from the bathroom and sprayed in the direction of every interior corner. He sprayed into the trashcan by his desk for a continuous ten seconds while he looked at his Movado sport watch. Then, when he determined it wasn't sufficient, he repeated for another ten seconds. Rogelio pursed his lips and pretended to look out the window.

"Good job."

"You're welcome."

She stuck out her tongue as he passed by her desk to return the spray can to the bathroom.

"Can you tell your employee to put her deliveries somewhere besides my desk?"

"The roses? Those are yours."

"Miss Leah got a *Sancho*[1]?" Rogelio teased.

"Me? No. I don't have a boyfriend, either. What are you talking about?"

She pulled the little card off the holder and opened it. Someone had scrawled Hope You Die Whore in block letters. There wasn't a closing or a signature. She was disappointed it didn't have a punchline, like: Hope You Die Whore. Love, Ronnie.

She snorted to herself, threw the card in the trashcan, and tossed the vase after it.

"What did you do that for?" Erik griped.

"Somebody made a mistake."

"The delivery man said they were for Owers."

The door opened. A woman and a girl in a brownie uniform came inside. Frank and Mario were close behind. Mario eagerly introduced his niece and her mother to the team. Little Marie gave her pitch and asked if anyone wanted to buy Girl Scout cookies. Mario added that her troop was very competitive. They wanted to be top sellers.

The desire to be number one resonated with everyone. They opened their wallets in support of the tiny salesperson. Marie was so excited and said thank you. Her mother didn't need to remind her. At such a young age, she'd already learned to be kind and gracious. Leah emptied her purse and placed an order for four boxes of Thin Mints and two boxes of Samoas.

She had a vision of Beka, several years older, in a Girl Scout uniform. Her daughter skipped door-to-door and canvassed the neighborhood. Leah watched from the barred windows of a tower. Why was she alone down there? Her heart ached.

Then she saw her innocently approach a sleeping dragon's lair and raise the cast iron door knocker.

---

1. *Sancho*
    A lover that a woman has on the side. (Spanish)

TWENTY-FIVE

Injured Players Report

The Credit Union's annual holiday dinner was open to every area franchise dealership. Leah arrived half an hour after the doors opened and instantly felt underdressed. She easily found Prince Auto's table.

Gerald brought his wife. Housely and Mclanic the Advertising Manager sat next to them. Aldo brought his older sister. Henry didn't feel well, and his wife couldn't get a babysitter anyway, so they weren't able to attend. Tommy didn't show either.

Everyone had already gone through the buffet. Since there was a short line, Leah got up to fix herself a plate. She picked through some items on the charcuterie platter and moved on when someone pointed out Prime Rib at the far end. They had the most opulent smashed potatoes she ever tasted. One of the servers told her the recipe included truffle oil.

Managers from Prince Auto Plaza's main competitor were seated near the stage. Their dealership won the Credit Union's Partner of the Year gold cup. Leah spotted the Supermodel's ex-husband. She thought he resembled an orangutan in heat.

Although Gerald was sloshed, he vowed to beat their rivals next year. Melanie didn't think Housely paid her the attention she deserved, and told him so in the most explicit terminology. Their squabble drew attention from other tables. Leah decided to leave after the awards ceremony ended. It wasn't fun to be the only sober person at a party, and she didn't want to get tipsy because she had to drive. She said goodnight to Aldo's sister and Gerald's wife. Then she made her getaway.

She took the elevator to the ground level and got out. The valet retrieved her loaner truck, and watched with concern as she pulled all the door handles from force of habit to check if they were still locked. Embarrassed by his stare, she tipped him five dollars and hoped it was adequate. When she got in, she pressed the electric door lock button three times consecutively.

She dropped her head.

Why am I doing that?

She didn't really know her way around the downtown area. Most of the streets were one-way so she paid very close attention. As she pulled into traffic, she flipped on her headlights and looked for signs. El Paso's iconic Star on the Mountain lighted the way and helped her get her bearings. She was so focused, she didn't notice the full-size sedan pull away from the curb and trail her to the house.

PRINCE AUTO PLAZA'S holiday celebration was an extravagant affair held in the conference center wing of a local hotel. It was one week after Thanksgiving. Three weeks before Christmas. The company lavished gifts and door prizes on merry employees. Leah wore a sparkly royal blue dress with matching shoes, and rhinestone barrettes in her hair. She was ecstatic when she won one of three diamond tennis bracelets. A salesman won a trip for four to the Super Bowl. Several employees made off with plasma TVs and Sony PlayStations.

Jolly Old Saint Nick made an appearance. So did Tommy Prince and his son, Jimmy. The teenage heir apparent groped Leah's left breast in an awkward moment on the crowded dance floor. In a millisecond, she burned with the inclination to lecture him about life. She wanted to tell him, in The Book of Proverbs, a female named Wisdom coached young men about masculinity and responsibility. The same Wisdom counseled her pupils to avoid sexual misconduct, mob mentality, drunkenness, and dishonesty. Instead, Leah took the easy route. She overlooked his miscalculation.

General Manager Will Housely placed a wooden gift box on the open bar, removed its lid, and gently lifted the treasured bottle of Macallan scotch. He refilled his whiskey glass all night, but it didn't dull his senses. Rather, as the evening progressed, the aged spirit fueled his lust. He eyeballed the banquet hall for every display of decadence and descent into depravity. Employees who came up to express gratitude found him to be preoccupied and taciturn.

Shelley and Bulldog Ben dirty danced as Stalwart and Nick eyed each other from different tables. Three ladies of the evening invaded the company party, and Brittany bumped into one near the restroom. After a few seconds, they remembered their acquaintance. The prostitute told her Housely paid her and two others to entertain the unaccompanied males.

Leah and Flor walked arm in arm for much of the

evening, which prompted the Elvis impersonator to ask if they were dykes. Valerie brought her husband, and talked excessively. Leah could smell alcohol on her breath. Jake chose not to attend the party.

ON MONDAY, Leah heard some new stories. Yermo had been attacked by two men in an alley. The reason for their dispute was unknown. He received several stitches and didn't show up to work the rest of the week. Howard the Fleet Manager and his wife Doris stayed in a room at the hotel after the company party. An ambulance whisked him away in the middle of the night. Hospital experts diagnosed him with liver damage from Hepatitis C. He was in intensive care.

Bulldog Ben swore a midget was the last person he saw before he blacked out early Sunday morning. When he awakened in his apartment, both of his nipples were pierced with miniature barbells and he had pain on his rear hindquarters. He asked Chen, his roommate, to look back there and tell him what he saw. After Chen recovered from the hysterics, he described a bad tattoo of a ginger mustachioed gunslinger with a hair-trigger temper. The character pointed six-shooters at a pair of bunny ears that poked out of its hiding place. The rabbit hole was positioned precariously in the crevice between his cheeks.

At an opportune moment, Leah took Ben's hand and quietly led him back to the body shop. She introduced him to Flor, who was a recovered alcoholic. Flor and Ben talked for a few minutes and she invited him to her congregation's AA meetings. They'd hosted those for the past several years and touted the best bagels and lox in west El Paso. She promised it wouldn't interfere with his work schedule. He said he'd have to think about it.

A few afternoons later, Leah visited white-haired Howard in his hospital room. She brought him a small vase of daisies and a happy face Mylar balloon. After they prayed, she left a book on his bedside table and gave teary-eyed Doris a hug.

On the way back to work, snowflakes fell and melted on her windshield. Leah turned at the post office to mail a music cassette. It was the sixties country pop single "Make the World Go Away." The special-order clerk at Blockbuster Music had told her it was in the bargain bin because no one ever picked it up. Leah thought it was a perfect gift for the Farmer, and would make good use of his new truck's cassette player.

When she got back to work, there was a large envelope on her desk. The contents were a holiday card and a check for seven hundred fifty dollars. The Farmer had kept his promise. The blue cover of the card read *Shalom*[1] and had the image of a seven-branch candelabrum. She noticed it wasn't the typical number a Hanukkah menorah would have. On each candle, there were names of Jewish feasts: Passover, Unleavened Bread, First Fruits, Pentecost, Trumpets, Day of Atonement, and Tabernacles.

She dialed the Farmer's number but there was no answer.

---

1. *Shalom*

   A word with many meanings, to include "peace" or "wholeness." (Hebrew)

TWENTY-SIX

Fiery Arrows

New Year's Day (1999)

I t was early morning in the employee lot. She listened to tropical steel drums and Jimmy Buffett lyrics about a safe harbor where children played. In one more month, it would be February. She'd found a nice little apartment nearby that was ideal for her and Beka. The rent was extremely affordable and her income had been steady. Any leftover money after bills and expenses would go into a savings account. She'd neglected it until now but she'd save a sum and invest in the stock market. Her wealth portfolio must increase. Revolving credit must decrease. She was eager to keep the promises she'd made to herself to be self-sufficient and ready for blessings.

It was time.

When the song finished, she got out and locked the car door. She wanted to pull all the door handles and check the trunk's latch, but she paused to pray instead. With a deep breath, she put one heavy foot in front of the other and walked to the main showroom. It was her morning routine to walk through and say hello before she headed over to her office at the Truck Center. On the way, she passed make-ready and waved at Jesús and his guys.

She saw Mr. Jameson on the used car lot. He left Melanie the Advertising Manager and went inside. Melanie thoughtfully approached the hood of a silver midsize sedan, dangled an antique pocket watch on a long chain, and waited. A holographic gargoyle with onyx eyes leapt out of nowhere. It perched on the thin woman's shoulders and back. Stony claw fingers stirred perilous smoke circles into her scalp. The conical pendulum mimicked haltingly, as if the Laws of Creation resisted.

The infernal figure let out a prolonged shriek, or at least Leah thought so until she realized her own vocal chords emitted the scream. The hologram curled its lip at Leah and vanished into black fog. The sleepwalker next to the used car came to. The hologram didn't return. With a heartbeat like a rock and roll drum solo, Leah quickened her pace.

Housely and Stalwart stood in the sales tower[1], seemingly unconcerned, as their unseeing eyes looked through the windows toward used cars. Mr. Jameson was exasperated, there could be no question about it. He adjusted his belt buckle and shirt cuffs repeatedly. Leah had seen his twitch a few times, especially when a Finance Manager made his customers wait too long.

"What'd I miss?"

"Melanie wants to consult dead spirits."

"Why'd she want to do that?"

"She's checking the karma."

"Karma?"

"Every pre-owned car had a previous life."

"Reincarnation? For cars?"

He gritted his teeth.

She sympathized with the veteran sales pro, but her biggest concerns were for Melanie. Leah's instincts had hit the nail on the head, once again, with spooky accuracy. What she'd witnessed outside was an advanced level of divination, not some beginner's experiment with the Ouija board. Melanie probably felt alluring, powerful, and in total control. In truth, she was a pussycat, indentured to the force of darkness that preyed upon her mind.

Give her eyes to see.

THE YOUNG LATINA receptionist waved Leah over to remind her a few female employees had won a special prize at the company party: mimosas and a limousine ride to the hair salon. They decided they'd go that day. It was the beginning of a new month and the company expected business to be slow.

She reduced her voice to a whisper and told Leah that a few other female employees would take advantage of the overall lethargy and go to lunch as a group. They'd consult with an attorney, and they wanted her to join them. Leah glanced at the sales tower and saw Housely without his headphones. She didn't know how much sound the recordings picked up around the reception desk.

"Careful," Leah cautioned as she squeezed her co-worker's hand. "The acoustics are really amazing in this place." She held out her cell phone as a hint before she walked out of the building.

LEAH ENTERED the Truck Center in the nick of time to see an insurance agent slide an envelope across the desk to Erik. She was acquainted with the greasy little character. He promised Managers a kickback for every car buyer who switched over to his carrier. The one hundred dollars was a product of the way he overcharged new policyholders. Her co-manager slid the money into his top center drawer, and met her gaze. She cast him a disappointed look. He averted his eyes and closed his desk drawer shut.

That reminded her of a new development in the dealership's bird-dog[2] payment policy. The office wouldn't send any more referral checks in the mail. Finance Managers now paid out the fees cash-in-fist[3] after referral customers signed their contracts. The new process was to sign out petty cash from the cashier, and staple a copy of the receipt to the front of the deal's purchase order. Managers, not sales consultants, determined when a customer was a true referral. The word of a sales consultant wasn't worth anything because they'd abuse the system at every opportunity. No one bothered to audit the Managers' decisions.

Since she became a Special Finance Manager, sales consultants frequently offered to pay her to help their credit challenged customers. Gerald was brilliant at his job, but he couldn't always get their customers done with his list of lenders. She refused the bribes, and chose instead to assert herself during Save-A-Deal meetings. When she offered to assist on a troubled credit deal, Gerald openly mocked her lack of experience and disregarded her suggestions. He clearly didn't want to be upstaged. She had to tiptoe around his ego to get a peek at the problem deal jackets[4].

During one Save-A-Deal, Gerald made her look like the biggest dunce when he said she wanted to partner with Tommy and become a female car dealer. Billy Bruce must have told Gerald she'd asked questions about the dealer development program. She received fire from every direction. Negative commentary ranged from, "Sugar, you don't have what it takes," to "Do you know what a Columbian necktie is?" Even Erik said he wouldn't want to bother with the headaches, or jump through the manufacturer's every hoop.

She wanted to stop, drop, and roll into the fetal position but maintained her composure.

AROUND LUNCHTIME, the receptionist called Leah but the call went directly to voicemail because she was with a client. She had two consecutive appointments after that, so she didn't retrieve her messages until much later. As she walked to the showroom in the burnt orange glow of sunset, on the way to do her daily ritual, she held the phone to her ear and listened.

"It's Chuck. I stumbled on to some information while I was at the county courthouse. Your customer's story about Molek Motors has been bugging me, so I looked them up. Molek has two DBAs: Prince Used Cars, and Prince Auto Imports. The documents have Housely's signature at the bottom. But, beware, that doesn't mean it's a legitimate Tommy Prince enterprise. What it does mean, though, is Molek Motors can cash checks made to Prince Used Cars and Prince Auto Imports because Tommy has never claimed those DBAs."

Leah's head swam. She reached for the closest new car to regain balance.

"Do you understand what this means? Call me."

She pressed the button to save the voicemail message.

The next one was from the receptionist.

"I know you're busy. If you get a chance, call us at this number. We have an appointment at one o'clock. The office is on Yandell."

Leah's heart pumped with alarming rapidity. Her thoughts screamed at her to run far away from there. A sharp dagger of panic pierced her. She began to hyperventilate and fought to control her breaths as she clutched a purse to her chest. When she felt the need to retch, she dodged between two cars and hid. Customers and sales staff would judge her harshly if they saw her, so she wanted to keep her private battle from scrutiny as much as possible.

Her female co-workers caused a predicament for her when they drew a line in the sand. If she joined their lawsuit, each woman's career including hers would blow up in the path of destruction. If she didn't join them, she could stay in the game and try to fix the dealership from within. Troublemakers would certainly lose in the long run. She decided to care more about her and Beka's future than what might happen to a few misdirected women.

LEAH NEVER FELT SO DEMORALIZED. Housely said she couldn't leave the dealership or go home at the end of a day without his consent. He sent salesmen to the Truck Center at random times to check on her. They followed his instructions and snapped photos with a disposable camera. The incessant click of the flash and winding of film drove her bonkers. If she wasn't behind her desk, she had to find someone who could vouch for her whereabouts. Other Managers didn't have to ask permission. They pulled up their big boy pants before they went to buy a pack of menthols or bubble gum at the gas station.

Daddy, may I go on a tampon run?

Then anonymous threats came. Not the comical Hope You Die, Love Ronnie variety. An outside call was transferred to her extension and a robotic voice said it would slice her throat. A series of pornographic faxes had her name written on the images.

On a Saturday morning, she was first to arrive so she unlocked the Truck Center door. Her drawers had been ransacked. Sensitive documents from deal jackets were scattered on the floor. Feminine products were strewn across her desk with the emptied boxes on display. It took half an hour to reorganize, and she refused assistance from co-managers. Whether someone had a copy of her desk key, or they'd jimmied the lock, didn't really matter. She was weary and desperate for peace of mind.

Two deep creases formed between Erik's eyebrows as he watched his friend suffer.

---

1. sales tower

    Term used to describe where the sales managers sit when penciling deals.
2. bird-dog

    A fee paid for a customer referral.
3. cash-in-fist

    Payment in paper currency.
4. deal jacket

    A folder that contains all the information in a customer's transaction.

TWENTY-SEVEN

The Old Man

Far away from Leah's persecution, the breakfast crowd had already begun to thin out at the Clock restaurant. A grey cowboy carried a large manila envelope and strode past a Please Wait to Be Seated sign. He parked himself in an available booth by a window. No objection from the haggard server who sauntered over from the counter. She poured a cup of steaming coffee as he delicately set his Resistol straw hat upside down on the table. He thanked her kindly, and requested the special with two eggs over-easy. She went off to put in the order.

He removed the contents of the envelope and lay the documents before him. Next, he unclipped a thin, black barrel from his shirt pocket and set it to his right. Finally, he put on his wire rim reading glasses. He breathed steadily as he flipped through and carefully read each page. He paused for a few moments and reached for a white cotton handkerchief with which to dab his moist eyes and blow his nose. Then he folded and tucked it away, read-justed his eyeglasses, and returned to the important task. He was able to make quick work of it. By the time his server arrived with a hot plate of Tex-Mex, he waited with a pleasant, worn smile.

When the old man had finished his meal, he left two twenty-dollar bills and tipped his hat at the server on his way out. He got back into his pickup and placed the manila envelope on his dashboard. After half a minute, the truck exited the lot and merged into traffic.

A lone Sentry on the roof of the restaurant watched him drive away. She looked to Heaven, made a deep curtsey, and followed the cowboy.

TWENTY-EIGHT

Underwater

Leah plopped on the couch in the customer waiting area as Housely worked on Silke's car deal. She must find a way to work through recent issues and win back his trust. She'd been naïve. Even though she answered to Tommy, Housely was her number one. She hadn't reached anywhere near his level of autonomy. He'd been a dealer principal and traveled in his own jet airplane; she simply aspired to be one of the jet-set while she continued to drive to work in a rusty beater. Housely was her superior in every aspect of the car business. Tommy depended on Housely to monitor dealership fixed and variable operations when he was away. She didn't even know how to interpret a spreadsheet, much less speak intelligently to stakeholders about the numbers. Leah had to admit it to herself: she could use a lesson or two from the master. No matter Housely's past mistakes or current misdeeds, without the Pax Romana, she didn't have a snowball's chance in Hell.

Housely said he'd come for her when he was available. She scooted herself over the couch and settled beside the soothing ambiance of the aquarium. The burble of running water. The murmur of an air pump. Striped fish with pink eyes darted around the tank. A stalk of artificial seaweed waved slowly in the bright light. An angelfish floated upside down. Cloudy eyes and rapid flutters of the gills indicated an imminent demise. Its ragged fins brushed along the rocks.

After fifteen minutes, Valerie told her Housely awaited her upstairs in Tommy's office. Since he was on a trip, Leah reasoned that would be an ideal place for them to sit and hash things out. As smart as she thought she was, the daydreamer was oblivious to The Devil's schemes. In her haste to make a deal at the front door, she'd been careless and left the backdoor open.

When she walked into the dim office, it smelled of extinguished candle wicks but she couldn't find the source. Housely sat forward in Tommy's black leather wingback chair. He pointed for her to sit in the chair across from him and his fingers resumed to tap on Tommy's desk. Betty, Housely's sister, was a shady form in a guest chair by the closed drapes. The Comptroller remained a mute observer.

Of all the underhanded conduct Leah witnessed in her brief time at Hell's Auto Plaza, the following six minutes trounced them all. With his elbows on Tommy's desk and his fingertips touching in agreement, Housely presented a case that Leah Owers had been derelict in her job duties. He strung together a list of accusations based on spurious information and specious testimony from those who would remain unnamed. The room tilted and an omnivorous shadow swelled behind him as he weaved a litany of allegations: inappropriate relationships with subordinates and employees from other departments; not a team player; difficult to work with; frequently mishandled cash;

contracts were rife with forgeries. Intolerant of the pantheon and alternative lifestyles.

The coup de grâce: The treacherous woman attempted to lead others to join a lawsuit against the organization that paid her a living wage. Her disgrace was a foregone conclusion. He wasn't interested in an answer. He boomed that he regretted his decision to hire her. Leah's mind reeled with several retorts about her oppressor's guilty stains, but she held her tongue. Any insights she revealed could potentially harm someone she cared for. She didn't know how he could actually believe anything he said; it must be personal. At long last, her contempt for his shadow grew so great she collapsed into bitter tears.

Housely terminated Leah, effective immediately. Texas was an at-will employment state. He informed her she was ineligible for rehire and the company's attorney would file a temporary protection order by the end of the day. If she didn't keep her distance, the legal battle would cost her in more ways than just financial. He assured her he represented the wishes of Hell's Auto Plaza and Tommy Prince.

The decision was final.

TWENTY-NINE

Upside Down

Housely escorted Leah off the premises. She didn't want to go but she turned off her cell phone, tossed it into the front passenger seat, and drove north. As she took Route 54 through the desolate landscape into New Mexico, she tried to think of something, anything, she could have done or said to save herself. It wasn't until she passed a small range of hills around the barren community of Oro Grande that her intense humiliation surrendered to mourning.

She hurt as if she'd had a significant loss. It wasn't about the job or the income, or the slight increase in status. She'd miss those things too, but it was more intimate. It was as if she'd merely skinned her knee but a surgeon broke the tragic news that he'd have to amputate. She hadn't told anyone about her five-point plan, but she might as well have. So much for the desire to achieve her loftiest dreams, or provide the best kind of life for herself and Beka. Say *adiós*[1] to the influence and ability to make a substantial difference. She grieved that others could impede her progress with impunity.

What could she have done differently?

She wasn't guilty of what Housely accused her of, but she wrestled with the knowledge that she wasn't above reproach. For instance, she took revenge on Carlos. Whatever he did or didn't do, she should have just let it go. Her own pride blinded her.

She figured she tripped the wire and set off Housely's alarm in a couple of ways with her attempt to intimidate Arturo. Number one: she shouldn't have cast Melanie as the priestess in her fictional narrative. Housely may not have even heard that part; his poker face was notoriously deceptive. Number two: she inadvertently gave Arturo a mic to gossip about rat-face's felony conviction. Nevertheless, she was certain Housely still didn't have a clue she was aware of his recordings.

She punched Henry in the nose to save Timothy from a traumatic experience. Her protective instinct shifted into high gear and it was unavoidable. No one ever said anything about it but, even if they knew, it wasn't as if Henry was held in high esteem. The other Managers often ignored him as if he were a stepbrother with Attention Deficit Disorder.

Unfortunately, Aldo resented her. He thought she'd reported his drug abuse, which she didn't, and that she'd stabbed him in the back to get the boss man to notice her. Erik often quarreled with her like a sibling, but she believed he genuinely cared. She got a lump in her throat and forced herself to check off a mental list of all the other employees who may have been her anonymous accusers: Frank, Gerald, Stalwart, Shelley. Service, parts, body shop, the office. Betty, Melanie. Sales consultants. Receptionists. Lot attendants. Make-ready. Jake. She had to consider the possibility that everything Housely declared was an utter lie.

She was adrift, prohibited from contact with numerous friends and acquaintances.

Housely could be cruel. He often kidded that he saw dollar signs in sales consultants' eyes. It was a Freudian slip. He was the one with a sliding scale, which he used to estimate others' net worth so he could gouge them. People were debits to his checking account, or assets he could sell at maturity. But, to her, they meant so much more than that.

Stalwart's advice in the interview had been: "Be so valuable they can never replace you." Since that moment, Housely had drawn a double-underline at the bottom of Leah's column and she was in the red. As good as a bad check about to bounce. It didn't matter that Tommy was pleased about the revenue she brought in last quarter. Clear strings pulled taut until there was a personal rift. To Housely, she was underwater[2] and upside down[3].

Her tear ducts were dry and she was numb.

LEAH STOPPED for gas in Alamogordo, resumed the drive north, and turned east onto US 82 before La Luz. The Tempo puttered steadily as the two-lane highway inclined into the Sacramento Mountains. She headed toward Lincoln National Forest. She didn't need a map because she'd been there before. The last time she'd traveled through, her church youth group leaders took turns behind the wheel. Young Leah and several zany teenagers were packed into the rickety 15-passenger van. They'd spent an unforgettable week at Aspendale Summer Encampment and she'd heard Father's voice for the first time.

When she arrived in the snow-dusted village of Cloudcroft, she parked behind one of the charming shops and got out of the car. The scent of Ponderosa pine welcomed her return to a higher altitude. The hint of fresh baked bread drifted by. Her nostrils breathed in the calming smells as she retrieved her down jacket from the back seat.

The shopping district was relatively sleepy for a weekday afternoon. She thought it might be due to a holiday hangover. Her cold fingertips dug into deep pockets as she stepped lightly on the mixture of melting snow and forest floor debris.

A bubbling brook trickled within range, so she walked in that direction.

An ancient melody of singing needles and rustling leaves swept the tree line in search of a lover's harmony. The top branches of towering pines stretched skyward and swayed. She shivered slightly and gazed into the clear blue. This was what she was made for.

When she got to the water's edge, a gust of air hushed the hair out of her eyes. A warm glow enveloped her shoulders and exalted her head. She tossed aside rebellion and reluctance like a pair of ill-fitting stilettos. The Craftsman accepted her metaphoric bare soles on consecrated ground. It felt as if nothing could come between them. He said her life was a beautiful thread He would hand knot into a livable design. The broken, thorny path didn't ruin the plan; He'd remove her stains. In awe, she soaked in His vintage for hours until she felt the fullness.

Sentinel 2 waited for his charge with respect. He came into her peripheral vision once but, when she glanced over, she didn't see anything by the clump of wild trees.

During Leah's return trek down the mountain, her lesson was reinforced with an amusing postscript when bonding glue gave way and her rearview mirror fell off. She laughed aloud, and instantly recalled a verse from summer camp: "Forget the past and reach forward like an athlete across the finish line."

Upon her return to El Paso, she parked in front of the house and turned her cell phone back on. It was a few minutes after 10 p.m. Refiner's fire may have depleted her physical reserves, but her peaceful soul was heartened.

HELL'S AUTO Plaza mailed Leah a whopping last paycheck of eighteen dollars and forty-two cents. To say her emotional response was righteous indignation would be an understatement.

When TWC (Texas Workforce Commission) investigated, the company asserted she made off with thousands of dollars of parts department special orders. To add injustice to injury, the dealership's official statement about the cause for termination was she failed to return to work. Apparently, no one saw Housely escort her off the premises. Carlos was promoted to Special Finance Manager, and readily attested to the alleged narcotics relapse which led to her absence. Every figment of their fabrication was reinforced with further sophistry. She doubled down on her unemployment benefits claim, and demanded to see the parts invoices. The TWC representative showed her the copies. Her forged signatures were at the bottom. TWC's initial decision was to deny, so she appealed.

Leah was dumbstruck by the ease with which Rat-Face Housely, High-Bangs Betty with the raccoon eyes, and Skinny Carlos disparaged her reputation. She knew the sulfuric pit where their spirits of animus had taken hold but she wondered how those afflicted by such could function, let alone appear to succeed in life. She concluded the trio, and many others at Hell's Auto, had uprooted and dissociated from absolute truth. The damage resulted from continual participation in The Devil's grift. Consciences were shriveled. Insight was corrupted. To them, evil was good and good was evil.

Her concerns about unemployment had yielded, but she was cognizant that she may never land another job in the car business if Hell's Auto was her only automotive reference. Legal representation crossed her mind, but she was strapped for cash. Her credit card account balance exceeded six hundred dollars; she refused to use the card again unless there was a legitimate financial crisis in her family. She knew she was destined to return to a restaurant job if she couldn't find a better option within a month. In hindsight, it was wise she hadn't pulled the trigger on a new car lease. She was thankful she'd delayed the lipo procedure.

Within two weeks of Housely firing her, as Leah pushed a stroller through the neighborhood park, an officer of the court served her with a notice. The official document was a temporary protection order. It specified she was to stay one hundred yards away from any company-owned property, which included all Hell's Auto retail locations.

She took it to the TWC representative, and he included it in her file.

SHE CONTINUED to talk with her friends but warned them not to call from the dealership because, as she phrased it, Housely's spies were everywhere. They were careful to stay off the dealership phone lines. She maintained a close connection to Erik, Flor, Valerie, and a few others. Jake left a brief voicemail the afternoon Housely fired her. He asked her to return his call, but she couldn't work up the nerve.

Flor called to report that Ben the Marine faithfully attended every AA meeting. He made a rapid adjustment to sobriety and was hungry for the public reading of Holy Script. To Flor's surprise, he volunteered to be an usher for the congregation's upcoming human trafficking fundraiser. She credited Father of Lights for the miracle. Leah rejoiced over the good news.

The Redhead, Gina as her closest friends knew her, contacted Leah to make a pregnancy announcement. Donald had stepped up to his responsibility and they'd gone to a counseling center. Although she'd leaned toward adoption, the memory of Leah and Beka the night of the tailgate party gave her hope. She felt inspired to keep her baby, and asked Leah to be the godmother.

Erik told Leah that Ronnie quit. Leah had never drilled him with questions about her because, from their conversations, he'd seen too many rookie-level baseball players with inflated egos cheat on their wives and quickly lose everything worth living for. When he told her Ronnie had been married all along, she was shocked. Ronnie never mentioned her marriage to anyone but him and Frank. Her husband, an oil worker in the Permian Basin, returned to El Paso for only one weekend every two or three months. They spent very few hours together and didn't have children.

Not long after Ronnie went to work at the Truck Center, she and Frank entangled in a steamy soap opera affair. She served her husband with divorce papers and packed all her belongings into a U-Haul trailer. When she arrived at Frank's house, he wouldn't let her in because it was the middle of the night and his daughters were asleep.

They argued on opposite sides of the screen door until she let out a bloodcurdling scream. That prompted next-door neighbors, who were also Frank's elderly parents, to call 911. The ruckus and the police scared the girls so much they wet their beds. Erik said that was the end of Ronnie and Frank.

Valerie told Leah that Tommy had been out of the office because of a legal matter. His son Jimmy was involved in a two-vehicle collision on I-10, east of El Paso. The highway patrol who arrived on the scene determined his blood alcohol level was .08. An ambulance treated him for minor injuries, but the driver of the other vehicle passed away at the scene.

Leah was cut to the heart because she'd had an opening at the company party to offer Jimmy a course correction but she'd chosen Money over Love. She felt terrible for the Princes. They'd likely fail to keep the story out of the news. She asked Valerie to leave a kind message on Tommy's desk. Valerie said she'd only learned about the accident when Tommy called and demanded to speak with the title clerk. He wanted to run a license plate search because the other driver's truck had his dealership's decal.

The deceased driver turned out to be David John Chapel. Leah dropped her cell phone and wailed when she heard the name. It was Mr. Chapel.

The Farmer.

---

1. *adiós*

    Goodbye. Literally, "to God." (Spanish)
2. underwater

    A term to describe the condition of owing more than a vehicle's worth.
3. upside down

    A term to describe the condition of owing more than a vehicle's worth.

Heir Apparent

Someone from Hell's Auto Plaza's main number called Leah's cellular phone. Must have been a mistake. Maybe her number appeared on the service assistant's daily task list, and the call was an attempt to schedule her next maintenance appointment.

She tried to remember if she'd forgotten anything. She knew the sales staff was under strict orders not to communicate with her under any circumstances. In the event a prospect or a customer asked for Leah, they were to keep their mouths shut and request assistance from an available Sales Manager. How difficult could that be?

Her phone pulsed once more and stopped.

One minute later, there it went again. Two calls in a row from Hell's Auto.

She relented. When she answered, she stated her name to alert the caller about their grave error.

"Ms. Owers, my name is James T. McEnany, Esquire. Did I catch you at a good time?"

She didn't recognize his voice, but she knew it must be a prank.

"Who is this again?"

"James T. McEnany. I'm calling from my law office in Midland. I apologize for the interruption. Your receptionist transferred me to your phone. Said she didn't know when to expect you at the office."

"James McEnany. Incoming calls are recorded. I'll need to call you back. What's your office number?"

He rattled off a series of digits that started with 432 and promised his phone call was in reference to an urgent matter.

She was surprised at how quickly he remembered the correct area code for Midland. She dialed the number just for kicks. A couple of rings.

"Law Offices of Smithson, McEnany, and Roy," a cordial female voice articulated. "How may I direct your call?"

Leah raised her eyebrows.

"Yes. James McEnany."

"My pleasure," crooned the associate who instantly transferred her.

"McEnany here."

"Mr. McEnany, I thought someone at Prince Auto Plaza was pulling a prank."

"Is that right? Just what kind of operation are you running over there in El Paso?"

"You don't want to know. Actually, I'm not an employee there anymore. Now, if you don't mind, what's this about?"

"Ms. Owers. My law office specializes in the area of Wills and Probate. David John Chapel retained my services prior to his untimely death. You probably knew him as Hank Chapel. I'm the executor of his estate."

"Yes, I knew Mr. Chapel. I think he lived alone. I don't

know if he had any relatives. I'm sorry, I didn't really know much about him."

"Don't worry, that isn't why I contacted you."

THE WINSOME ATTORNEY told Leah she was the sole beneficiary of the Farmer's estate. Since Hank Chapel didn't have any relatives, he doubted anyone would contest the will. Leah told him there must be a mistake because the Farmer didn't know her very well.

He reassured her Mr. Chapel had been no fool; he'd hired a P.I. to conduct an inquiry into her character. Leah was surprised to learn someone had followed her for several weeks without her knowledge. The attorney said the inquiry agent documented her activities at work, at the house, and a few other locations. There were photographs of incidents at the dealership when Managers mistreated her or other women, among many situations of daily life he was able to capture. She thought it might provide a group of ladies the evidence they needed for their lawsuit against the dealership, and requested the attorney send her the file immediately.

He told her probate usually took between six to twelve months. He explained, in that particular situation, the process might take up to two years. The decedent owned extensive property. There would have to be a complete appraisal of two plots of land, water and mineral rights, the house and other buildings, equipment, and every item of value. Two part-time employees continued to live rent-free on the central piece of land near the main house. If the estate tax or other taxes became a burden to the benefi-ciary, she could sell one or both plots of land later to cover it.

The rest was straightforward. There were no retirement accounts and no investments. No insurance policy. Mr. Chapel didn't owe any debts. His bank accounts had a combined balance of one hundred twelve thousand dollars. As the executor, he'd deduct any costs related to probate or other expenses from those funds.

He told Leah there was nothing much to do except wait. He'd be in touch and she could call anytime if she had questions or concerns.

THIRTY-ONE

Restoration

On a Sunday afternoon, Susie and Ralph surprised Leah with a small birthday get-together. They'd invited a few friends over to the house. Flor and Ben. Valerie, Jesús, and Jake. Erik and Leesa, and their baby boy. Chuck and Linda, and their gang of kids. Susie served green chile chicken *enchiladas*[1] and peach iced tea. Everyone contributed items for the potluck, and they ate their fill of comfort foods. Hannah and Sofia sang a song they'd written especially for Leah. After applause and hugs, they led Beka and the other children to the toy room.

Leah curled up in a rocker recliner and finished a decadent slice of cheesecake. She loved that the house was packed. The commotion all around filled her heart. Family and friends talked about a variety of subjects. Very soon, Hell's Auto Plaza became the main topic.

Erik, Jesús, and Jake mentioned their negative experiences and worrisome observations. She never thought she'd hear complaints from any of those men. There was solidarity in the living room about wrongdoing at the dealership. She was relieved everyone spoke so candidly with each other, and in front of their spouses. Flor and Ben listened from the kitchen as they helped Susie clean up.

Erik wanted to know about Chuck's new business, which had taken off much better than anyone expected. Since Erik was ready to leap to a new branch, they exchanged business cards and Chuck promised they'd discuss the subprime housing market over lunch after the month ended. Then Ralph took Chuck aside to inquire about Molek Motors' DBAs.

Valerie asked if she could talk to Leah on the back porch while Jesús surreptitiously steered Jake in the same direction. When they met by accident at the backdoor, Jesús grinned broadly and gently pushed Jake and Leah through. In no less than two languages, the matchmakers told the singles they were past due for a private conversation. To ensure the message got through, Valerie restated they would be alone for an hour and body language was permitted. She and Jesús went inside and clicked the door closed.

Leah and Jake blushed.

After a short pause, he asked her out.

HE TOLD her he was two semesters from a UT Law degree. His extended hiatus would end soon. The plan was to return full-time next fall. In the meanwhile, he dismissed every phone call from the Princes. They could find someone else to finish those repairs. He'd warned both Housely and Prince about the legal ramifications of audio recordings without disclosure or prior consent, but they repeatedly ignored his advice. Now that they'd injured his Leah, and he'd heard about her suspicions of further foul play, he'd distance himself from their slippery operation in perpetuity.

Jake's plan after graduation, hopefully within a year, was to pass the bar and start his law practice. He didn't want to live in El Paso, but Leah didn't want him to move too far away either. They wanted to take things step-by-step and enjoy life, and they also wanted to marry. She decided to tell him about the attorney's phone call.

Naturally, he had lots of questions.

"Where is the land located?"

"Three hours southeast of here. Before Fort Davis."

"How many acres?"

"Sorry, I didn't think to ask."

"That's alright."

"I was trying to wrap my mind around the news."

"The attorney said there were mineral rights?"

"Yes, and water rights because of aqueducts."

"You mean, aquifers?"

She laughed at her mistake.

"Is that the word? What's an aquifer?"

"I'll do some research and tell you what I find." His tone grew serious. "That attorney is the executor of the estate. He has a fiduciary duty to the beneficiary. If I were you, I'd request a list of monthly expenses. While you wait for probate, the least he can do is give you a tour of the land. I'd like to go with you. Will you let me set it up?"

"Sure, Jake."

"One more thing," he sighed. "Whatever you do, don't talk to Tommy or anyone who speaks on his behalf."

"Why not?"

"Jimmy is on the hook for manslaughter."

"What does that have to do with it?"

"Tommy will go to any lengths for his son. His attorneys will comb through Mr. Chapel's life and they'll find a way to prove he was the negligent party in the accident. Nothing will be off the table. If they can create a reasonable doubt of the criminal charge against Jimmy, they could open a way to a civil claim against the estate."

She hadn't even thought of that.

ON A SUMMER DAY, agents from the Federal Bureau of Investigation stormed an El Paso dealership and presented their search warrant. The document listed Racketeer Influenced and Corrupt Organizations (RICO) acts which were indictable under Title 18 of the U.S. Code: section 1028 "fraud and related activity in connection with identification documents," section 1341 "mail fraud," section 1343 "wire fraud," and section 1344 "financial institution fraud."

Also listed were offenses associated with a case under Title 11 for "dealing in a controlled substance or listed chemical."

Swirling air from the hot asphalt formed into a funnel. The dust devil lofted sand and debris into the portico. Hundreds of large carrion birds and winged monsters circled perilously close. Every accomplice and accessory lost an eye or a hand that day.

Law enforcement didn't permit anyone to leave until they were cleared to go. Employees and customers were trapped inside the main building for two hours. The huge, clear panes became an odious porthole as flames licked the glass and black smoke billowed from showroom entrances. Shrieks and groans reverberated. El Paso F.D. trucks didn't roll in, but an ambulance came for a morbidly obese tomcat who'd had an acute stroke.

A barefoot *señorita*[2] sat cross-legged on her Tempo's hood. She'd parked at the busy strip mall across the street, and was the one person with eyes and ears to witness the underlying mayhem.

Any megalith that bore the Prince name didn't guarantee an everlasting legacy. Materials wore out. People eventually died. Bank accounts closed. Only stories were timeless. The aether thumped with a classic rock anthem about losers and champions. She kissed her index finger and pointed it to the blue sky.

FBI agents led an enraged General Manager away in handcuffs. At his arraignment, a felonious record didn't help. He was judged a flight risk and bail was set at seven figures. Other arrest warrants were pending.

Almost relegated to a footnote, an indictable act under Title 18 separate from **RICO** wasn't officially addressed but an anonymous caller tipped off the local press. News reporters had a field day about a confiscated suitcase full of cash and section 2511, "interception and disclosure of wire, oral, or electronic communications."

Automotive customers called a hotline and formed the first civil class-action suit against the Prince family crime syndicate.

---

1. *enchiladas*
    A rolled tortilla with a filling, typically meat, served with a chili sauce. (Spanish)
2. *señorita*
    An unmarried woman. (Spanish)

THIRTY-TWO

The Tour

Jake Tanner parked the rental in the driveway. It was a large white SUV with room for eight. He and Ralph loaded the overnight bags. Susie and her daughters clamored into the back as Leah attached Beka's car seat to the center row. She checked her purse and diaper bag once more to make sure she hadn't forgotten anything.

"Let's roll," Jake announced.

He'd arranged to meet with McEnany in two hours. They'd cut it very close.

Everyone buckled in and shut their doors. As the SUV entered I-10 East, the sisters played their Connect 4 travel game and shared cheesy goldfish crackers with cousin Beka. The men debated politics from both sides of the aisle. Jake said he thought Bush's son would run for president, but Ralph doubted he'd be able to win a debate against the V.P.

Susie quizzed Leah about her plans. TWC finally approved the unemployment claim so she had room to breathe. Leah wanted to savor every moment with Beka before she returned to full-time work. She also didn't want her past year at Hell's Auto to add up to nothing. Susie encouraged her to apply at a few local car dealerships and find what opportunities were out there. Leah agreed it couldn't hurt.

Part of her still intended to enter a dealer development program. The banker told her he knew of several dealer principals who mentored candidates and helped them get a franchise of their own. Maybe she could work out a deal with an owner operator in Texas to acquire their franchise, or persuade them to invest in hers.

She felt the Farmer's estate was a godsend. If the land would be valued at two million dollars or more, it would give her leverage and she'd be taken seriously as a business-woman. McEnany had told Jake the two plots combined were over 30,000 acres and explained why the aquifers were so valuable. The oil industry thirsted for water resources in the arid Permian Basin. Leah could easily find a water developer who would pay her a royalty to produce and sell millions of barrels of non-potable fracking water.

The property virtually paid for its own costs.

AT NOON, Jake pulled into a gas station a couple of clicks west of the I-10 and I-20 interchange. McEnany was already there and he waved out the window of his blue pickup. They stopped for gas, a bathroom break, and a diaper change. Ralph bought bottled water for everyone. Then the SUV followed the pickup out of the parking lot and into highway traffic.

Several minutes later, they passed the I-20 junction but exited I-10. They stayed on the access road and McEnany called Jake's cell phone to tell him the fenced land on both sides of I-10 at that point belonged to the estate. They turned right at a paved county road and McEnany continued the guided tour over the phone.

They proceeded a little slower now. The fenced land on both sides of the road also belonged to the estate. A large spring fed trophy bass lake glistened in the sunlight to the left. Several cows grazed in the pastureland on the right. Small and large green hills offset the rocky crags in the distance.

Susie gasped and pointed out her window. Her girls and Leah marveled at the sight. A herd of aoudad rams rapidly rounded one hill and went up to the ridge overlook. Beka gurgled with delight as she played with a plush toy.

After two or three minutes, they turned left at the front gate of Chapel Ranch. A friendly worker held them there to wait for a mother partridge and her chicks to cross, and then he waved them through. The huge two-story stone house with large porches and two smaller residences beckoned to them. A series of rocked in ponds decorated the front yard. The landscaping was in meticulous shape.

Leah unbuckled Beka, took her out of the car seat, and exited the SUV. She held her daughter's hand under open sky and gazed at the boundless splendor, speechless. Her betrothed put his arm over her shoulders. Their eyes locked, and the realization hit them both simultaneously. They were home, and it was a blessing beyond reckoning.

The rest of the family gathered around and, aside from joyous tears, only the chirping, rustling, trickling refrain of creation could be heard because none cared to trespass the palpable, hallowed hearth in their midst.

THIRTY-THREE

Promised Land

Four-year-old Beka Tanner giggled. She ran a short distance behind her two older cousins along a dirt path to the largest of three lakes on Chapel Ranch. Forty meters from the water's edge, Beka kneeled to tie her shoelaces. Her skin radiated a warm glow. A delicate breeze hushed the hair away from her face. She raised her head, and spoke with boldness. Her cousins turned to look and listen. They could see and hear only Beka's side of her conversation with the luminous Emissary.

Her Daddy was at the law office, fighting for justice. Her Mommy was in the lake, teaching people how to be superheroes. Mrs. Flor was at the big house, showing survivors how to live. *Señor*[1] Jesús said she could play with the lamb—after she finished her chores.

- She didn't see any fat cats,
- top dogs, or
- blowhards anywhere.
- No one was hungry-for-more in that *hacienda*[2] of abundance.

- There were no such things as tyrants.
- Zero carnal Christians.
- No instigators hidden in the tall grass.
- Nary a prejudiced tribunal within sight.
- Best of all, slander beyond the fences was too far away to be heard. Even if it weren't, it didn't matter. *YHWH*[3] showered His favor on her every day.

Beka stood with her feet far apart in the sand and her arms crossed. With a dazzling smile, she hopped three times and waved at her otherwise invisible friend.

"*Toda raba*[4]!"

With that, she skipped away to join her stunned cousins.

"Blessed are you." Matthew 5:3-11

---

1. *Señor*

    Mister. (Spanish)

2. *hacienda*

    A large estate of land, especially for the use of farming or ranching. (Spanish)

3. *YHWH*

    The four letters of the holy name of God: Yod, Heh, Vav, Heh. These are consonants, not vowels. Some believe it is pronounced "Yehowah" with a breathy emphasis on the h's. Experts differ about the precise pronunciation, and whether or not it should ever be uttered. However, there is universal agreement *YHWH* would not want His name said in vain. (Hebrew)

4. *Toda raba*

    Thank you very much. (Hebrew)

Epilogue

24th of *Thammuz*[1], 5761 (July 15, 2001)

The light-bearing agent floated to an aerial view of the water, glided toward the divers, lingered a moment, then lifted off slowly. The lake diminished below as treetops, hundreds of creosote bushes, roofs of houses, specks of cattle, and green hilltops came into view. Those fell away, and white cumulus curtains closed in.

The beatific figure's ascent intensified. He shot into the stratosphere, transcended to the main outpost, and peered down through the clear sky dome.

A SINGULAR ARC OF LIGHT, barely perceptible, stretched from southeast Texas to remote islands in Southeast Asia.

Special ops liberated hundreds of girls and boys from their heinous captors.

Other illumined arcs also spanned from Chapel Ranch. To a Hunter: a Firefighter in Lower Manhattan on September 11. To other Hunters: U.S. soldiers deployed to Iraq and Afghanistan. To a former Ballet Dancer from El Paso: founder of an underground liberation team in Eastern Europe. To the Supermodel from Austin: owner and pilot of a single-engine aircraft, and frequent traveler to South America. To Gina and Donald, and their generations: non-profit relief workers in Africa. To Linda and Chuck, and their generations: entrepreneurs, software company execs, and charitable mega donors. To Leesa and Erik, and their generations: investors, owners of a pro sports team, and major political supporters.

A multiplicity of colorful strands branched out from the source beams. They flourished and graced the perishing planet. It was afternoon on The Sixth Day.

Decades fast-forwarded through elections, civil war, market scarcity, and infection. Orthodoxy underwent deconstruction. Satraps and other officials blotted out appellants by decree. Tech society built barriers that divided families. Digital mediums reprogrammed orphans. Opioid sorcerers cast sleeping spells.

Evening fell, and The Day arrived. A bolt of electrons orbited once around Earth. Thousands of rose gardens blossomed and a million chrysalises matured into monarchs. Church lamps ran out of oil. $YHWH^2$ made a deliverance covenant with twelve tribes of young Daniels. They hadn't defiled themselves with sexual immorality, and were qualified, blameless testifiers of Truth.

In every person's native language, Sky Messenger 1 announced the imperative to worship Maker-Creator.

When Great Babel buckled, Sky Messenger 2 relayed the news.

Lawless 1 regulated remuneration for global citizens, desecrated the Sacred Trust, and murdered two Proclaimers. Erstwhile, Sky Messenger 3 warned people not to receive the beastly Imprint nor bow to False Hero.

In the seventh year of the seventh millennium, Exiles united in defiance against Beast of Prey. Anthropomorphic arms interlinked. Resolute rescues with new names, devoid of collar, leash, or microchip, gathered under darkening skies. Back limbs of those spayed, neutered, and intact alike became intractable as tree roots. Mass euthanasia ensued, but whirlwinds of dandelion puffs and down feathers couldn't be contained. Turbulence grew... until... scarred human feet of fearsome majesty touched down. The King of kings, Master of the universe, impacted a mountain. A wellspring erupted from the cleft.

He was compassed by mobilized Multitudes, and flanked by Heaven's Forces. His Word was their sword. Vile, winged creatures crashed to the ground. Blood splattered the landscape and *HaSatan*[3] was chained. False Hero and Beast of Prey were trampled and incinerated.

The people of *Yisrael*[4] led *Melo HaGoyim*[5] into *HaAretz*[6]. They waved palm branches and cried shouts of *Hosanna*[7]. Young Daniels followed *Meshiach*[8] wherever He went, and sang a new *Hallel*[9] from a mountaintop.

Peace and righteous government reigned. A four-year-old girl played Follow the Leader with a calf, a lion cub, and a lamb. Fresh fruit of the vine flowed at every feast. People shared the histories around annual bonfires.

A fleeting shadow turned the pages of a final exam... The seat of judgment issued its last subpoenas... Then...

HAOLAM HABA[10].

---

1. *Thammuz*
   The fourth month of the Jewish religious year. (Hebrew)
2. *YHWH*
   The four letters of the holy name of God: Yod, Heh, Vav, Heh. These are consonants, not vowels. Some believe it is pronounced "Yehowah" with a breathy emphasis on the h's. Experts differ about the precise pronunciation, and whether or not it should ever be uttered. However, there is universal agreement *YHWH* would not want His name said in vain. (Hebrew)
3. *HaSatan*
   An alternate name for The Devil. Literally, "The Satan." (Hebrew)
4. *Yisrael*
   Israel. (Hebrew)
5. *Melo HaGoyim*
   Fullness of the nations. (Hebrew)
6. *HaAretz*
   The Land [of Israel]. (Hebrew)
7. *Hosanna*
   Expression or adoration, praise, or joy. (Hebrew)
8. *Meshiach*
   Messiah. (Hebrew)
9. *Hallel*
   A prayerful recitation of Psalms 113–118 on Jewish holidays as an act of praise and thanksgiving. (Hebrew)
10. *HaOlam Haba*
    The coming world. (Hebrew)

Did the story or any of the characters resonate with you?

Connect with the Author and be the first to know when she has any cool news to share with her Readers' Group.

For my beloved son.

JOSHUA

December 11, 1993 - July 14, 2020

Connect with the Author and join her Readers' Group!
COUNT ME IN

250

Glossary

A

A la una y media
At 1:30. (Spanish)

abuelita
Familiar name for a grandmother. (Spanish)

ACV (Actual Cash Value)
Wholesale value assigned to a vehicle at trade-in, based on
guides and estimated cost of reconditioning.

adiós
Goodbye. Literally, "to God." (Spanish)

B

barrio
Neighborhood. (Spanish)

bird-dog
A fee paid for a customer referral.

Buenos tardes
Good afternoon. (Spanish)

buried
A term to describe the condition of owing much more
than a vehicle's worth.

business office
Slang used to describe the area or office where F&I
managers work.

C

CPO (Certified Pre-Owned)
A used vehicle that has been inspected and refurbished by
the dealer.

Call Until They Buy or Die
An old saying from management to salespeople.

carpe gallus
Seize the rooster or cock. (Latin)

Carretera Federal 83
Federal Highway 83 in Mexico. (Spanish)

cash-in-fist
Payment in paper currency.

Cerro Bola

Name of a mountain in Mexico. Literally, "ball hill." (Spanish)

chiqui
A common nickname that could mean several things including shorty, cutie, or little girl. (Spanish)

chola
A young woman belonging to a Mexican American subculture commonly associated with street gangs. (Spanish)

Ciudad Juárez, México
City of Juarez, Mexico. (Spanish)

close
Term to describe the act of convincing a customer to agree to a sales transaction.

cockroach
Slang term used by old school salespeople to refer to bad credit customers who they feel are wasting their time.

Code four
An attractive female.

cojones
Courage. Literally, "a man's testicles." (Spanish)

Cómo estás
How are you? (Spanish)

compadres
A traditional term to describe mutual reverence and

friendship, often between a child's parent and godparent. (Spanish)

crème fraîche
A dairy product similar to sour cream or Mexican crema. (French)

D

DMS
Dealer Management System software.

DMV
Department of Motor Vehicles.

deal jacket
A folder that contains all the information in a customer's transaction.

ducks on the pond
Customers on a car lot.

due bill
A document to describe work promised or outstanding obligations.

E

El Chuco
Nickname for the city of El Paso. (Spanish)

Ellos son hermanos
They are brothers. (Spanish)

enchiladas
A rolled tortilla with a filling, typically meat, served with a chili sauce. (Spanish)

F

F&I
An acronym for Finance and Insurance.

first pencil
The opening offer from a sales manager, often written onto the four-square worksheet.

five-pounder
A sales transaction with a gross profit of five thousand dollars.

fútbol
Soccer. (Spanish)

G

H

HaAretz
The Land [of Israel]. (Hebrew)

Habla usted inglés
Do you speak English? (Spanish)

hacienda
A large estate of land, especially for the use of farming or ranching. (Spanish)

Hallel
A prayerful recitation of Psalms 113–118 on Jewish holidays as an act of praise and thanksgiving. (Hebrew)

hammer
Slang used to describe putting hard pressure on someone.

HaOlam Haba
The coming world. (Hebrew)

HaSatan
An alternate name for The Devil. Literally, "The Satan." (Hebrew)

hat trick
Slang used to describe selling three cars in one day.

Hola
Hello. (Spanish)

Hosanna
Expression or adoration, praise, or joy. (Hebrew)

I

ikigai
A concept about direction or purpose that makes life worthwhile. Literally, "reason to live." (Japanese)

Isla Navidad
Name of a place in Mexico. Literally, "Christmas Island." (Spanish)

J

jalapeño
A very hot, green chili pepper used in Mexican-style cook-
ing. (Spanish)

Jawohl
Yes, absolutely. (German)

K

L

La Biblia es la Verdad. Léela.
The Bible is the Truth. Read it. (Spanish)

lay down
Term used to describe a customer who signs on the very
first offer.

M

MSRP
Manufacturer's Suggested Retail Price.

machaca con frijoles y queso
Description of a burrito filled with marinated skirt steak,
onions, peppers, tomatoes, and chilis. Topped with beans
and cheese. (Spanish)

Melo HaGoyim
Fullness of the nations. (Hebrew)

ménage à trois
An arrangement in which three people share a sexual relationship. (French)

menudo
Traditional Mexican soup made with beef tripe in broth with a red chili pepper base. (Spanish)

Meshiach
Messiah. (Hebrew)

modus operandi
A well-established method of doing something. (Latin)

Momma's boy
A male customer who needs a parental co-signer to get approved.

money that Momma doesn't need to know about
An unofficial cash payment that doesn't leave a paper trail.

Muchas gracias
Thank you very much. (Spanish)

Muy bien
Very good, or very well. (Spanish)

N

negative equity
A term to describe the condition of owing more than a vehicle's worth.

Nisan
The first month of the Jewish religious year. (Hebrew)

No problemo
No problem. (Spanish)

Norteño
A style of folk music associated with northern Mexico and Texas, typically featuring an accordion and using polkas and other rhythms found in the music of central European immigrants. (Spanish)

O

OEM
Original Equipment Manufacturer.

over the curb
A sales transaction that has been completed and the customer has driven the vehicle off the lot.

P

P.O.
Purchase order.

para mañana
For tomorrow. (Spanish)

Peor
(In the Bible) The name of a mountain peak in Moab, mentioned in Numbers 23:28, to which King Balak led Balaam in his fourth and final attempt to induce him to pronounce a curse upon the Israelites threatening to occupy his land. The heresy of Peor is the event recorded at Numbers 25:1–15. Later biblical references to the event occur in Numbers 25:18 and 31:16, Deuteronomy 4:3, Joshua 22:17, Hosea 9:10; Psalm 106:28. New Testament references are found in 1 Corinthians 10:8 and Revelation 2:14. Literally, "open wide." (Hebrew)

peso
A basic monetary unit of Mexico. (Spanish)

picadillo
Description of a burrito filled with lean ground beef,
tomato, potatoes, and spice. (Spanish)

pico de gallo
Fresh salsa made from finely chopped ripe red tomatoes,
white onion, jalapeños, cilantro, lime, and salt. (Spanish)

precaución
Caution. (Spanish)

Puente Internacional Córdova de las Américas
Cordova International Bridge of the Americas. (Spanish)

Puente Libre
Free Bridge. (Spanish)

puto
An insult to anyone perceived to be weak or contemptible.
Also an expletive. (Spanish)

Q

quid pro quo
An exchange of goods or services. (Latin)

quince años
Fifteenth birthday. (Spanish)

R

raison d'être
The most important reason or purpose for someone's existence. Literally, "reason for being." (French)

ranchera
Songs that originated on the ranches and countryside of rural Mexico. (Spanish)

roach coach
A blue collar catering truck.

S

sales tower
Term used to describe where the sales managers sit when penciling deals.

salsa verde
A tart sauce made from tomatillos, chili, and cilantro. Literally, "green sauce." (Spanish)

San Patricio
A village in Jalisco, Mexico. Literally, "Saint Patrick." (Spanish)

Sancho
A lover that a woman has on the side. (Spanish)

Se Habla Español
Spanish is spoken. (Spanish)

Señor
Mister. (Spanish)

señorita
An unmarried woman. (Spanish)

Shalom
A word with many meanings, to include "peace" or
"wholeness." (Hebrew)

silver hair
Car buyers who are senior citizens.

skate
A term used to describe when a customer is stolen from
another salesperson.

sold lane
A spot a salesperson will ask the customer to park after a
test drive, as a soft close technique.

sotto voce
Sung or said in a quiet voice, as if not to be overheard.
(Italian)

split
A term used to describe when the commission on a car
deal is divided up between two salespeople.

stroke
Time-wasting shopper.

strong
A term used to describe a salesperson who closes a high
percentage of car deals.

T

T.O. (turn over)
Philosophy to never let a customer walk out the door without management intervention.

tacos
A traditional Mexican dish consisting of a small, folded corn or wheat tortilla topped with filling. (Spanish)

telenovela
Latin American serial drama similar to a soap opera. (Spanish)

test drive
Driving of a motor vehicle to determine its drivability or roadworthiness, and general operating state.

Thammuz
The fourth month of the Jewish religious year. (Hebrew)

Toda raba
Thank you very much. (Hebrew)

tortas
Mexican sandwiches. (Spanish)

tortillas
Round, thin, flat breads of Mexico made from unleavened corn meal. (Spanish)

trade walk
A term used to describe when a salesperson takes the customer around the trade vehicle and silently examines its flaws.

tranny
Colloquial name for "transmission."

U

underwater
A term to describe the condition of owing more than a
vehicle's worth.

up
A customer who walks on the lot.

up point
A place where a salesperson stands to wait for the next
customer who walks on the lot.

upside down
A term to describe the condition of owing more than a
vehicle's worth.

V

W

weak
A term used to describe a salesperson who cannot close
any of his own deals and hasn't sold anything yet.

X

Y

YHWH
The four letters of the holy name of God: Yod, Heh, Vav,

Heh. These are consonants, not vowels. Some believe it is pronounced "Yehowah" with a breathy emphasis on the h's. Experts differ about the precise pronunciation, and whether or not it should ever be uttered. However, there is universal agreement *YHWH* would not want His name said in vain. (Hebrew)

Yeshua
The name of a beloved rabbi born approximately two millennia after Abram son of Terah. Crucified by Roman soldiers and died on a hill the same moment the Passover lamb was killed for Temple sacrifice. Literally, "salvation." (Hebrew)

Yisrael
Israel. (Hebrew)

Z

Copyright Notice

About the Author

Edie Roskam is a 20-year veteran of automotive retail in the southwest US and a connoisseur of Korean foods. As a single mother with a full-time job, she earned an online Business Administration degree without trading her sanity. She has also worked at a music store and role-played in a job interview for a super secret government agency. These days, she and her rockstar-superhero husband Patrick rescue canines. They reside near the Sandia Mountains in New Mexico where faraway echoes of ancient peoples may be heard on starry, summer nights.

9 798519 081856